She had to make her position clear

"Clay," she said suddenly, "I'm going to tell my father that there's no way you and I can simply take up where we left off. I think it's best to tell him straight away, despite his illness, don't you?"

Clay didn't answer for a long time. Then he said evenly, "That's up to you, Melly."

Melly thought for a bit. "I should have thought it was the only thing to do from both our points of view. Nothing's changed between us, has it?"

"If it has, we'll never know now, will we?"

"But nothing *can* change your reason for marrying me, can it? The fact that you and my father have forgiven each other doesn't alter us."

He didn't reply, and she didn't expect him to.

LINDSAY ARMSTRONG

saved from sin

Harlequin Books

TORONTO • NEW YORK • LONDON
AMSTERDAM • PARIS • SYDNEY • HAMBURG
STOCKHOLM • ATHENS • TOKYO • MILAN

Harlequin Presents first edition July 1985
ISBN 0-373-10806-0

Original hardcover edition published in 1985
by Mills & Boon Limited

CHAPTER ONE

MELISSA FORRESTER stepped out of the lift and surveyed the plush, thickly carpeted passage that stretched away to left and right like a river of rich, silky green. Elegant brass lamps glowed softly beside each panelled door, highlighting the expensive damask wallpaper, and a discreet, gold-lettered board indicated that numbers fifty to fifty-four were to the left and numbers fifty-five to fifty-nine were to the right.

Melissa grimaced and turned right to head for number fifty-nine. She'd checked her credentials with the doorman downstairs, whose main concern had been that she wasn't selling anything, but then some demon of perversity had prompted her to start from the top floor of this apartment block rather than the first floor which she usually and methodically did.

Perhaps, she mused, this urge to go about things upside down has something to do with the fact that it's a cold, wet, miserable day and not the kind of day one should have to be tramping the streets to make a living?

'Anyway,' she muttered to herself, 'it's not as if I'm going to get much of a response. You never do from these high-class addresses.'

This was something she'd discovered over the last three months since she'd been working for a firm that conducted opinion polls on a wide range of products. It was far easier in the middle to lower class suburbs to find people prepared to sit down and answer a series of questions about toothpaste and cornflakes. In fact it was not only easier but it often led to the offer of a cup of tea and quite often she found herself the unwitting recipient of some unlikely confidences.

But in areas such as the one she was working today, it was not only hard to find people with the time or patience to go through the routine, it was not even all that easy to find people home.

All the same as she approached number fifty-nine, she patted her conservative raincoat into place, checked that her shoes and tights weren't muddy or splashed, and smoothed her shining, wheat-fair hair. She was a girl of just below average height, on the thin side of slender perhaps, and with a trick of looking at the same time younger and older than her age, which was twenty-two. This curious fact about her was hard to pin down but most people took her for about nineteen – until they looked into her eyes. Then they stopped to wonder. But the bone structure of her small, oval face was beautiful, and most people found themselves strangely touched by her.

Not that she herself gave her looks much thought—although she was more smartly dressed today than her usual attire of jeans and an anorak because she'd found that to be better dressed gave her a better chance in more exclusive areas. Not, for that matter either, that she had a great choice of better clothes, but then she never saw the same people twice so it didn't matter.

And she made sure her clip-board was hidden in her large bag—another trick of the trade she'd discovered. Establish a presence first, her employer always said. Then get down to business . . .

She pressed the bell of number fifty-nine.

There was no immediate response. She waited for about a minute, then pressed it again and heard a muffled voice saying, 'Coming!' And what sounded like muffled laughter.

It was a further minute before the door opened and a girl stood there. An exquisite creature with a mane of tawny, disordered hair and a pair of laughing green eyes. The other thing that distinguished her was that she was wearing a man's shirt clutched about her and half-buttoned up crookedly so that it wasn't hard to guess that she had nothing on beneath it.

Melissa sighed inwardly, any doubts she'd had about it being one of *those* days banished. Days of polite and not so polite refusals for a variety of reasons—such as being caught in bed with a lover, she thought ironically. Well, perhaps that's being a bit hasty, she amended to herself, it is fairly early ... but its none of my business anyway!

All this passed through her mind speedily so there was only the briefest pause before she said with a practised smile. 'Hello. I'm Melissa Forrester and I hope I haven't disturbed you but I was wondering ...' She stopped abruptly as the tawny-haired girl's mouth dropped open and a look of incredulous, stunned surprise widened her green eyes.

They stared at each other for a long moment. Then the other girl closed her mouth and licked her lips. 'I ...' she hesitated. 'I don't know what to say.' Her voice was attractively husky but curiously lame and embarrassed sounding at the same time, and as if she realised it, she shut her eyes briefly and swallowed visibly. Then she turned her head and called softly over her shoulder, 'Mike . . . I mean,' she winced, 'well . . . you'd better come. There's a visitor for you.'

'No!' Melissa was galvanised into speech. 'You don't understand. I'm only here to ask you about . . .'

But she didn't go on because a tall, dark-haired man had appeared behind the girl, and he too was buttoning up his shirt. But he stopped as his rather hard, surprisingly light grey eyes flickered over Melissa, who was standing transfixed. And that same look of stunned, shock flared in them as it had in the girl's. Then he blinked and said, 'Hello, Melly. This is a surprise . . .'

But it seemed that what he found surprising was more so for Melissa. Because, before her fixed gaze the doorway and the two people it framed began to whirl alarmingly, and the floor no longer felt solid beneath her feet and she crumpled to it soundlessly as she fainted for the first time in her life.

She came to slowly, afraid to open her eyes in case the world was still behaving so alarmingly. But she realised dimly that she was half-sitting, half-lying on something soft that had the texture of crushed velour beneath her fingertips, and that there was an aroma of brandy around her, and that the front of her precious new, lavender-blue jumper felt damp against her skin. And that someone was saying urgently, 'Should I call a doctor?'

Her eyelids fluttered open and she found herself staring upwards bewilderedly, to see that the tawny-haired girl was dressed now, in fashionable knickerbockers worn with long leather boots and a bright orange fun fur. And for all that she was not as young as Melissa had first thought, and for all that her clothes looked as if they'd been thrown on and a hasty comb dragged through her hair, the effect was still stunningly attractive. But those green eyes were concerned and anxious.

Melissa said raggedly, 'No! I'm fine.' She sat up and tried to stand up but a strong hand held her back.

The tawny-haired girl frowned. 'Look,' she said awkwardly, 'I'll go out. No, Mike . . . I mean, oh hell!' she groaned exasperatedly. '*Look*,' she went on wearily, 'I've got an appointment in an hour or so, anyway, so don't worry about me. I . . .' she paused and her green eyes searched Melissa's face, 'I can only say I'm awfully sorry,' she finished quietly, and walked out of the room.

Melissa stared after her, then she glanced around the room, taking in the bright, clear colours—the white, velour-covered lounge suite that was stunning against a sulphur yellow wall-to-wall carpet and pale, moss green walls. Gold framed paintings hung on every wall, vibrant with every colour under the sun, pinks and turquoises, dark blues and red-browns and although some were still-lifes and some portraits and some impressionist scenes, they all bore the same strong brushmarks of the same painter.

Melissa drew her brows together as if something was niggling at the back of her mind but, whatever it was, it refused to dislodge itself from her subconscious, and she turned her head at last to the man sitting beside her.

'Why does she keep calling you Mike?' she asked helplessly. 'Did you change your name too . . .' She broke off abruptly and a faint tinge of colour flared briefly in her pale cheeks.

'No, Melly,' Clayton Forrester said dryly. 'She

calls all her lovers Mike. So you did change your name when you ran away? I thought you must have,' he added.

The silence was broken only by the patter of raindrops on the windows and Melissa wanted to tear her eyes away from his grey ones but found she couldn't. And she tried to think of something to say but it was as if her mind was deadened by a sense of shock that was almost too great to bear. Then finally, she heard herself saying foolishly, 'She seemed rather nice.'

Clayton Forrester studied her critically for a long time, her face, her hands that were nervously clenched in the lap of her simple grey skirt, her hair that was pinned up today in a no-nonsense knot and a fleeting expression of pain tightened his mouth. But he said almost immediately, 'Thank you. I suppose one should be flattered when your wife approves of your ... mistress, for want of a better word.'

Melissa shivered inwardly at the irony in his voice but was at last able to look away. And she drew a deep breath and when she looked back at him, her eyes were faintly wry as she said, 'I haven't been your wife for a long time now, Clay. Did you expect me to be horrified to find you with another woman? It wasn't that you know. I got over that ages ago. It was the shock of seeing *you* again. Because that was something I'd vowed I'd never willingly do.'

A spark of something like anger lit his eyes but all he said was, 'Oh?'

'Yes. You see . . .'

'Melly,' he interrupted harshly, 'you may like to think you're not my wife but technically, you are still.'

Melissa regarded him thoughtfully. And found that he'd changed hardly at all. There were some lines beside his mouth she didn't remember but that was about it. His body was still lean and powerful and his features unblurred. Clayton Forrester was not handsome—at least that's what you thought and found yourself admitting in the same breath that he was wildly attractive, however. And part of that attraction undoubtedly lay in his tall, finely knit body. Yet there was more to it. There were certain contradictions about him that were part of it too. His mouth was well cut and seemed to indicate a quality of almost monk-like asceticism but his eyes often discounted this. Sometimes they were cynical and mocking, sometimes lazily amused and if you were a woman they could, as Melissa had discovered, look you over fleetingly so that your rate of breathing accelerated unaccountably and you were left with the curiously uncomfortable but at the same time rather dizzying thought that monk-like was not a good way to describe Clayton Forrester. And the thought that had followed, in Melissa's case, had been equally uncomfortable but less dizzy-making. It had been that only someone very special probably, lovely and mature and intelligent, oh, very special, would make the grade with him, as a companion or a lover or a wife. Because added to everything else about him, he had an air of almost saturnine cleverness that was not open to dispute.

No, she thought, no-one could deny that. He's very clever, sometimes diabolically clever. But that's not my problem any longer . . .

'Am I still your wife—technically speaking?' she said, her words following hard on the heels of her last thought. 'I wondered about that. I thought you might have divorced me by now. I think you can do it—in absentia—if your spouse disappears for long enough. And it's been nearly three years.'

His eyes probed hers but she returned his look steadily and enquiringly. 'No,' he said at last. 'I didn't. But tell me something, how come after changing names, you've reverted to using my name again? At least that's what you used just now, I gather.'

She grimaced. 'I needed to prove I was a married lady to get this job,' she said candidly. 'I work for a company that conducts opinion polls. Today I'm working on radio programmes—which is your favourite breakfast one and so on. That's the only reason I knocked at your door—life's queer, isn't it?' She half-smiled at him, her eyes which could darken to violet, reflecting the lavender-blue of her jumper.

'Very,' he agreed. 'But it's not my door. It's Tanya's.'

'Oh.' Melissa glanced around the room again and frowned faintly. But she said, 'Is that her name? It suits her.'

He smiled grimly. 'Yes. It does. But to get back to what we were discussing—why did you need to prove you were a married lady? Especially,' he said ironically, 'since you've displayed such an aversion to being, as you put it, a married lady. I'm surprised you bothered.'

She grinned at him. 'So was I,' she admitted. 'But the job really suits me and I think they prefer married women because they're more reliable. When you've been out of the workforce for a long time, as many married women have, you find it hard to get any kind of job, so the ones you do get, you tend to persevere at. I think that's my employers' philosophy on the subject anyway. Mind you, I wasn't exactly the kind of married lady they go for. They told me they preferred *older* married women—as if they didn't quite believe it any way. But when I produced my marriage certificate, they capitulated and since then I've become one of their star canvassers.'

'Weren't you ... afraid that could lead to discovery?'

'Yes,' she admitted, 'for a while. Well,' she hesitated, 'to be honest, I'm not as cautious as I once was, so I took a gamble that not everybody in Australia would know who Clayton Forrester was, or even if the name did ring a bell, wouldn't have cause to connect me with *the* Clayton Forrester anyway, just think it a coincidence of names. I was right, it seems. Besides I thought you—both of you—probably wouldn't be still looking for me after so long.'

He stared at her so fixedly, she began to feel nervous again and she started to say something but he broke in.

'Melly ...' Her name was barely a savagely expelled breath and Clayton Forrester, the only person in her entire life who had persistently called her that, looked suddenly tortured. 'You didn't have to do this ...'

She looked at him gravely. 'Don't feel sorry for me, Clay. I'd hate that more than anything else you did to me.'

'You didn't ... hate everything I did to you,' he said after a long pause and watched her carefully.

'No,' she conceded and her eyes were clear and unshadowed as she returned his scrutiny. 'But I hated the motivation behind them. I always will. Well,' she said, 'that's that! I've had some surprising encounters in this job but none as surprising as this. They do say life is full of coincidences, don't they? And you have to admit this has been a most amazing one . . .'

'*Has* been?' he shot at her.

'Yes,' she answered calmly, and looked around for her bag and raincoat.

But he put out a hand as she made to stand up and restrained her. 'If that means what I think it means, Melly,' he said abruptly, 'I have to tell you you're in for a shock.'

She eyed him steadily. Then she said evenly and without anger, 'Let me go, Clay. We have nothing more to say to each other. Besides which, I still have fifty-eight apartments in this block to canvass.'

'No,' he said with barely concealed menace. 'If you think you can walk back into my life like this, and then walk straight out of it again, you're mistaken.'

'I'm not mistaken,' she said coolly. 'I'm not anything you like to call me. I'm my own person now. I come and go when I please and there's nothing you can do to stop me.' She pulled her arm free and stood up.

He didn't follow suit but lay back and observed her critically. Then he took a swig of brandy from the glass he was still holding before putting it down on a side table. 'You've grown up,' he murmured. 'I don't know if I like it.'

'Who *cares*?' she said defiantly, for the first time betrayed into an attitude that was not as calm and philosophical as she'd have liked it to have been. And to her chagrin, she saw that he realised it, and his lips twisted into a slight smile and his eyes mocked her.

She bit her lip and turned away to pick up her coat and bag from another chair. But when she turned back it was to find him on his feet and a prickle of apprehension ran down her spine because he looked so tall, and she knew that if he chose not to let her go, there wouldn't be much she could do about it.

She said uncertainly, 'Clay . . .?'

'Melly?' he replied politely. But his eyes hardened at the look of confusion on her face. 'Oh, come on!' he said impatiently, and the glance he cast her was more than impatient. It was angry and ironically incredulous—the kind of glance that told her that he didn't suffer fools gladly. 'You have to admit,' he said through his teeth, 'that we have some unfinished business between us.'

She took a fortifying breath. 'You mean the divorce? Of course! I agree—it's silly not to get it out of the way. Let's see,' she paused, then said briskly, 'I'll give you the name of my solicitors— the firm of Lawson and Birchleigh . . .' She stopped, realising with surprise where the name came from. Lawson and Birchleigh were the name of the firm who handled anything of a legal nature for the company she worked for. I just hope to God they handle divorces, she prayed. Not that there's much to handle these days. In fact we could probably do it by mail . . .

'That wasn't what I meant,' he said tersely. And added abruptly, 'Have you seen your father lately?'

A nerve jumped in her jaw. 'No.'

'Have you never wondered . . . how he was?'

'I don't know why you're bringing him up . . .'

'*Have* you?' His words shot through hers like bullets.

'I . . . I'm sure he's quite fine,' she said coolly, after the barest hesitation. 'As a matter of fact,' she went on, 'I have seen him recently. In a picture in a newspaper. Like you,' she said with some irony, 'he didn't look to have changed much. And from the caption to the picture, I gathered he'd just made another spectacular business coup, so I don't suppose he has.'

'He's gravely ill, Melly,' Clayton Forrester said very quietly.

She looked at him blankly. 'He . . . can't be. It was only a few weeks ago that I saw the picture. Anyway, how would you know?'

But he ignored her question and said, 'I saw that picture too and I'm afraid there are some things about a man in a hat and an overcoat that don't come over too clearly in a newsprint picture. Nor is he advertising the fact of his illness. It's not the kind of thing you do lightly in his position because it can lead to a lot of potentially harmful speculation. I don't suppose the fact will become generally known until he's tied up . . . any loose ends.'

Melissa sat down abruptly. 'That ill' she whispered. 'Is he going to die?' Her voice rose a little. 'You wouldn't tell me this if it wasn't true . . .?'

His lips tightened. 'No, Melly. I admit I have some faults but . . .'

'Then how do you know all this?' she interrupted. 'If it's not public knowledge, why do you know? I thought you hated each other—I *know* you hate each other! He wouldn't have confided in you!'

'As a matter of fact, he did,' Clay said curtly. 'About a month ago he contacted me and invited me down to Glen Morris.'

Melissa's eyes were huge. 'He did that?'

'Melly,' he sighed suddenly, 'yes. And he told me about this condition he's contracted. And how he was very much afraid it was the end of the road for him.'

Melissa stared upwards mutely.

'He also,' Clay went on with a frown in his eyes, 'told me that he only had one thing left to live for. You—and how desperate he still was to find you. And that he didn't care,' his lips twisted slightly, 'how you came back to him, even as my wife. In fact he'd be happy for you it that's the way it was. But I had to tell him that I'd never been able to track you down either. In fact, all I could promise him was that if by some miracle, you did walk back into my life, I'd take you to him.'

Melissa closed her eyes. 'I . . . every year I sent Ellen a Christmas card, just to let them know I was all right. I . . . used to take a train trip to go as far away as I could in a day, to post them . . .'

'He showed them to me. It made me a little angry.'

Her eyes flew open to find him looking at her very directly. 'You're surprised,' he said harshly. 'Did you honestly believe I'd get any pleasure from the thought of you out in the world alone, adrift, hurt . . .'

'I . . . no,' she whispered.

'Then did you think you were punishing me that way?' he said through his teeth.

She gasped. 'No!'

'Then you might have included me on your mailing list, Melly,' he said tightly. 'It might just have saved me some sleepless nights.'

'You didn't have to have me on your conscience, Clay.'

'Well I did,' he said savagely. 'I'll always have you on my conscience. I . . .' He stopped. 'All right,' he said wearily, 'let's not get into that. But you do see why I can't let you just walk out of here, don't you?'

She licked her lips. 'I can go to him on my own. You can trust me.'

'Forgive me,' he said coolly, 'but I'm not going to take the chance. For nearly three years you managed to evade a virtual horde of people looking for you—mine and your father's. That was no mean feat and I don't intend to take the risk of it happening again. Running away seems to be something you're particularly good at, Melly,' he added grimly.

'I . . . oh!' she cried in a bitter, goaded voice. 'Were you so surprised that I ran away, Clay? Did you honestly expect me to stay to be nothing but a pawn between you and my father? For your part, a tool for revenge, and for his part to be treated like a silly, thoughtless *child*, and heaped with recriminations. Who could live with that? I certainly couldn't. But now it seems, incredibly, that you expect me to admit I was in the wrong. Yet the only wrong thing I did,' she said passionately, 'was to get caught up in a war I didn't even know existed!'

He stared at her and she suddenly saw some changes in him that she'd missed earlier. A sort of drawn quality about his eyes and a few strands of silver grey in the thick darkness of his hair that had not been there before. But then he's . . . thirty-five now, she thought inconsequently. Maybe they'd have come anyway.

'I don't expect you to admit that,' he said at last. 'But what you call the "war" between me and your father is over now. I have no wish to go on conducting a feud with a sick, maybe dying man who is desperate for his only child. That's why I made the promise to him that I did. Surely even you must see that I have to keep it? *Especially* you. Or is it that you're more like him than you care to admit, Melly?' he said softly. 'It took him long enough to lay down his arms—it took the thought that he might be dying to even contemplate having anything to do with me. What will it take for you to forgive him—and me?' His eyes seemed to pierce through to her soul.

She sucked in a breath. 'I ...' she said distractedly, then tried to take a grip on herself. 'I forgive him,' she said. 'I forgive you too, Clay. I know what pain he caused you and—I too don't want to carry on a feud with a sick, maybe dying man ... who is my father,' she whispered and swallowed. 'But you must realise, both of you,' she went on after a moment, 'that I'm my own person now. That doesn't mean I won't give him all the support I can ...'

'I don't think that will be enough for him, Melly,' he said very quietly.

'What do you mean ...?'

'I mean he wants to see you back with me.'

She stared at him blankly. '*Why?*'

Clayton Forrester studied her bleakly. Then he looked away and said in a voice devoid of all emotion, 'He feels now that he was wrong to tell you what he did because he's sure now, so he said, that you must have loved me very much to have done this. He said—for a lesser emotion, she wouldn't have been so hurt. And he asked me what I would do if I ever found you again.' Their eyes clashed as he looked back at her suddenly. 'I said,' his voice was curiously uneven, 'that if I ever found you again ... I'd do everything in my power to make it up to you for all the—pain and suffering I caused you ...'

Melissa went still. Then she turned her head to look blindly out of the window. To realise belatedly that the rain had stopped and that there was even pale sunlight coming through the windows, and a vista of clear, clear blue sky. But Melbourne's like that, she thought inconsequently. It has the most erratic weather I've ever known ...

'But it wasn't like that, Clay,' she said softly. 'I admit I thought I was in love with you. But I was wrong just as Daddy,' she savoured the unfamiliar word on her lips, 'is wrong now. In fact he was right the first time. Life *is* really queer, isn't it?' she said again and tried to smile. 'He said then that it was only the kind of crush that nineteen-year-old girls are particularly susceptible to. And that was the truth.'

'Is there someone else?' The question was quietly spoken but it took her completely by surprise so that she stammered a little in replying.

'N-no.' But she recovered her composure quickly. 'No. There's no-one. Should there be? Are you trying to tell me I'd have to fall in love with someone else to know I was never in love with you?' She grimaced wryly. 'Was I such a fool in those days? That you would think that was the only way I could work it out.'

'I'll tell you how you were,' he said with a curious huskiness. 'You were very young and unbelievably sweet. And sometimes those lovely eyes looked at me with a wariness you couldn't hide and you reminded me of a little girl playing with matches and wondering when she was going to get burnt. And you never gave me any come-on, never used any feminine wiles—I don't think you knew any. And I don't think you had any idea that sometimes that in itself is a very potent attraction. And there was something else about you that touched me. It was as if you'd ... conditioned yourself not to expect too much and not only of me, as if you were very used to being ... lonely. And I fell for all that as much ... as the rest of it. I told you ... I tried to tell you ...' He sighed suddenly and turned away.

'But don't you see, Clay,' she said shakily after a long time, 'that ... I do accept that you were attracted too ... but essentially I *was* a little girl playing with matches. I think in our hearts we both knew that. And if I hadn't been ... who I was, I think you'd have told me I was playing with matches. You would have let me down nicely but let me know all the same that we were in different leagues. Because you must have known that my kind of attraction was—well, for you it was only a novelty.'

He turned back to her and started to speak but stopped abruptly as if he'd changed his mind. Then he said with a strangely remote look in his eyes, 'Why don't you see your father first, Melly?'

'I will see him. But that won't change anything ... between us. To get back together because of my father, or because you feel guilty, is a *worse* reason than the one you had for marrying me in the first place. No, Clay ...'

'You're crying,' he said.

'Yes. Of course I'm crying!' she answered, scrubbing furiously at her eyes. 'It's sad, the whole miserable business is sad. But that's life. I made a mistake, you made a mistake—he made one too.

It's no reason to go on making them though. And I will go to him—you must trust me,' she said desperately.

His mouth set in a hard, uncompromising line then and they stared at each other. 'Yes you will, go to him,' he said at last. 'Because I'll be taking you. Oh, you can forget about the rest of it—I had the sense not to bring you back as my loving wife. Although you might find it not quite as easy to convince him as you've convinced me that you don't love me. But that's beside the point. Take you to him I said I'd do, and I will.'

'Oh God!' she sobbed, 'don't you understand . . .'

She broke off at a sudden sound and they both turned convulsively.

Tanya stood there looking awkward. 'I forgot to take any money with me,' she said apologetically. 'I got a cab and then at the other end found I couldn't pay for it so the only thing I could do was come back. It's waiting downstairs. Clay,' her husky voice deepened, 'you should be shot!'

She walked into the room with her eyes fixed on Melissa's white, tear-streaked face. 'The poor girl fainted when she saw you and all you've done since, by the look of it, is brow-beat her so that she looks as if she's going to faint again. Men,' she said exasperatedly to Melissa and put her arms around her. 'Honey, don't look like that.'

And for some reason beyond Melissa's comprehension, she found herself clinging to Tanya even while she realised it was a wildly incongruous, ludicrous thing to do.

And as she wept into the other girl's shoulder and started to sneeze as the bright orange fur got up her nose, she missed the muttered exchange between Tanya and Clay, in which Tanya said, 'For God's sake go and pay for the cab. And why don't you take a walk at the same time? I'll look after her . . .'

CHAPTER TWO

IT was very dark, so dark that Melissa lay very still, grappling with a powerful sense of disorientation. She could picture the room she was in—every room of Tanya Miller's apartment made an instant, an unforgettable impression—but she couldn't work out which way she was facing or where the door was. And as her heart started to beat faster, she remembered that as a child she'd often woken like this in the depth of the night and experienced the same sense of disorientation even in her own, beloved bedroom at Glen Morris.

Don't panic, she warned herself. It will come to you. Just think a little.

She took a deep breath and reached out a groping hand to encounter a wall. That means the bedside table and the lamp must be on the other side, she reasoned and turned over. And with a sigh of relief, her wandering fingers encountered a table top and then the cool porcelain base of a lamp, and finally a switch that responded to her fingers to spring to life and cast a subdued, rosy glow over the room.

She looked around and had to smile wryly because the door was exactly opposite to where she'd thought it must have been and she was facing in the opposite direction.

She lay back and with a suddenness that hit her like a blow, she forgot the suffocating lack of direction she'd experienced and realised just why she was sleeping in Tanya Miller's spare bedroom as the incredible events of the previous day washed over her.

I don't believe it, she thought with despair. Why did it have to happen? How could fate be so cruel?

She lay for a long time staring at the ceiling blankly. Then, slowly and inexorably, and despite her efforts to stop it, her mind came alive with a jumble of images that she thought she'd cured herself of forever. She twisted her head on the pillow and bit her lip painfully but it was no good. Time was claiming her, taking her back and she couldn't fight it. Back to the day Clayton Forrester married Melissa Heatley . . .

But no, she thought desolately, it all started long before that. Those powerful forces that were to affect her so terribly had their roots way back. How had he known? she wondered. How had he known that Melissa Heatley had suffered from one great lack despite all her privileges? I didn't even really know it myself . . .

Melissa's earliest memories were centred on Glen Morris, a stately old colonial farmhouse and property in an historic area of New South Wales that included Yass and Gundegai, where the dog sat on the tuckerbox, and where great fortunes had been made out of wool. In fact the vast, rolling acres of Glen Morris still supported sheep although by the time Melissa was born, the Heatley fortune had considerably diversified since her ancestors had bred merinos and thereby started it.

And the clearest of her early memories were of a dapple-grey pony to which she was devoted, a blue cattle dog which was devoted to her, and the annual Yass Show.

She'd been taught to ride, not before she could walk, but young enough to win a ribbon at the Yass Show when she was seven and the Yass showgrounds were as deeply and vividly embedded in her memory as were the pony and the dog. She only had to close her eyes to hear the wind sighing through the tall, dark-green pine trees to feel again the crunch of pine needles beneath her feet, to picture the little, old-fashioned pavilion and the sheep pens, to see the white cockatoos that sometimes invaded the pines ... Oh yes, it was hard to forget the Yass Show because for years it had been the highlight of her life.

This then had been the world of the only child of James and Barbara Heatley, a beautiful old house, a dog and a pony, a devoted nanny, and once a year, the stomach-churning excitement of the show which in her estimation far outdid the excitement of Christmas. And the fact that she didn't see a great deal of her parents didn't bother her because she'd never known any different. Besides there were explanations for it—Daddy had so many business interests he was incredibly busy, and Mummy had the house in Sydney, and two other households besides, and a great many social obligations to attend to. And anyway, Melissa knew they loved her because they often arrived at Glen Morris unexpectedly and then she'd have a marvellous few days with them, although she did sometimes wonder why they rarely came together.

It was only when she was twelve and had been unwillingly consigned to an exclusive boarding school that she came to understand just what a famous name the name of Heatley was, and how rich her father was and socially acceptable. No-one had bothered to tell her this before, least of all her Scots Nanny, Ellen Mackenzie, an extremely forbidding looking spinster, with a heart, when it came to Melissa, as tender as it was unexpected but nevertheless, with very rigid ideas on the bringing up of children which did not include spoiling them or allowing them to develop outlandish ideas of their own consequence.

Melissa came to realise something else through her years at boarding school. That her parents weren't quite like a lot of other parents—in fact it would be more accurate to say they were quite different. But it was a difference that was hard to pin down. They never fought or argued, at least not in front of Melissa—they were always perfectly civil to each other. Yet more and more she began to see that that very civility was like a solid brick wall between them and when she looked back, she realised that they'd never been close, in a loving sense. And she worried about it a lot in her teens because she adored them both.

But in the meantime, her life pursued its usual course, boarding school where she learnt a lot about life that wasn't in the text books, and Glen Morris, that secluded haven to come home to and always the same. The dapple-grey pony was still there although honourably retired, and when she got over heartbreak for the blue cattle dog who'd died of old age, there'd been a new puppy to take its place and successfully worm its fat, baby little self into her heart. And always horses and the familiar faces of the people who worked the sheep station, many of whom she'd known since she was a baby.

Then, when she was sixteen, her mother was killed in a car accident. It was Ellen who arrived late one night at the school to break the news to her, Ellen who took her home to Glen Morris, Ellen who tried to comfort her. And because her father had been in Europe, and because, by an unkind trick of fate, his flight home had been delayed, they met for the first time only an hour before the funeral. Which had all but broken the slender hold she had on her emotions.

What did break it, though, had been the look on her father's face during the funeral service, in the dim, old Yass church—a look of intense suffering and remorse, and she'd found herself thinking as she wept, if he feels like that, why didn't he show it when she was alive? Why didn't they ever show any of how they felt? So that I thought they didn't feel for each other at all . . .

But the funeral had had a curious outcome. It had not been a big one for the sake of privacy but it had become so at the graveside in the lovely old church yard because Barbara Heatley had been well known and well liked, a real lady many people said, and many people had come from far and wide to pay their respects.

And suddenly a lot of people had realised that James and Barbara Heatley, whose lives due to their wealth and position had always attracted a lot of interest, had contrived to have one well-guarded secret—a daughter, and a beautiful one at that—so many said, at least. How had they managed to keep her so totally out of the limelight?

But by the time Melissa had been accosted by the press on several occasions, her father came to a decision that bewildered her and she hated, but was powerless to resist. He packed her off to a finishing school in Switzerland, saying it was only what he'd planned for her in any case.

She spent nearly two years in Lausanne and although she vowed to hate every minute of it, she didn't. But she never quite got over the sense of hurt at being sent away so soon after her mother had died when the only consolation she'd been able to think of was to be at Glen Morris, if not with him.

It had marked the end of a period of her life. It was not that she didn't love her father as much as ever but it was as if no amount of telling herself that he'd sent her away for her own good could quite take away that hurt of being desperately lonely and so far from home. And it was as if there was a growing fear in her heart that she too would one day be expected to be as self-sufficient as her mother had been, as her father obviously was.

Of course he came to see her frequently and on her seventeenth birthday flew Ellen Mackenzie over to spend a week with her. But nothing totally made up for those moments when she looked around at beautiful snow-covered peaks, at everything surrounding her, all of which was growing more and more familiar, but finding herself feeling frightened and inexpressibly lonely.

Then her eighteenth birthday came and a beautiful diamond-studded bangle arrived, delivered by hand from a famous Lausanne jeweller who'd selected it on her father's instuctions – telephoned instructions and she received a cable too saying he'd been delayed in New York but Happy Birthday anyway. And she rebelled. She sent him a cable back saying that if he didn't let her go home she'd never speak to him again.

It worked. Within two weeks she was back at Glen Morris and she spent one whole enchanted month taking up the threads of her childhood, before it hit her that she was no longer a child. That as much as she loved the place, she couldn't deny a growing urge to spread her wings.

But that had not been so easy to achieve although it had taken a lot less than two years to do it. In fact it had only taken one stormy interview with her father which she remembered almost word for word.

'Daddy, all I want to do is get a job in Sydney! What's so wrong in that?'

Blue eyes had stared into blue eyes, her's mutinous and stubborn, his angry and stubborn. 'You don't need to work, Melissa.'

'Yes I do! You can't expect me to languish away here until someone marries me!'

His eyes had sharpened. 'Is that what you're worried about? That will never be a problem, Melissa. The opposite will be the problem really.'

She'd set her teeth. 'It wasn't what I was worried about at all. I have no intention of getting married for ages. But I want to *do* something. I want to be independent and earn my own living, and for once in my life, live a normal kind of life like every other girl I know.'

A fleeting look of hurt had crossed his face and she'd winced inwardly because the words had slipped out and not been what she'd meant to say. But curiously, it had had the desired effect—to an extent.

'All right,' he'd said abruptly. 'You can come and live with me at the house in Sydney. I was planning that anyway. And I'll help you look for a job.'

'I . . . that wasn't what I had in mind,' she'd said quietly. 'I've been in touch with a school friend and she wants me to share her flat with her. I,' her voice had been a little shaky, 'would like to do that.'

'No.' The statement had been unequivocal. And the argument that had ensued fierce, during which he'd told her that he had no intention of allowing her loose to become prey for every fortune hunter in town, and she'd told him that he was absolutely Victorian in his outlook—always had been. 'But I'm *eighteen* now,' she'd said finally and added desperately, 'Anyway you can't stop me! I'll do it whether you like it or not. But isn't it stupid for us to fall out over it? And isn't it stupid for you to try and make me feel guilty about it? Don't we mean more to each other than that?'

'Yes,' he'd said finally and heavily. 'Yes, you're right. But you do see why I worry about you?'

'Of course,' she'd answered. 'But you can't keep me locked up in an ivory tower all my life. Look, I promise you one thing, I can't really say I won't marry or fall in love for ages but if I do think I'm in love, I'll apply the acid test. If it's someone who is broke and he wants me to elope with him, I'll know he's on the make.' She'd smiled through her tears. 'But if he's broke and he still wants to apply to you, then we'll know he's fair-dinkum, won't we?'

'And if he's wealthy but not . . .'

'If he's wealthy, then we'll know he wants me and not your fortune.'

'It's your fortune too, Melissa.'

'I guess so although it's . . . hard to visualise. But that would be a perfect solution, wouldn't it? For a very rich man to fall in love with me and for me to fall in love with him,' she'd said mischievously.

'Melissa, my dear, if I've given you the

impression that all I was concerned about was someone marrying you for your money, I didn't mean to. I . . . *foremostly*, I want you to be happy.' He'd looked at her with a frown of pain in his eyes.

'I know, Daddy,' she'd said softly. 'Trust me, a little though. I won't do anything stupid.'

How unprophetic, Melissa thought as she moved restlessly in Tanya's spare bed. My father was right, I should never have been let loose. In fact the only consolation I have is that I didn't fall for a fortune hunter. Oh no, I fell for something far more dangerous. But I didn't know . . . how could I have known? And let's not go through all that, *please*.

But her overwrought brain disobeyed her and took her back . . .

Two months after returning from Switzerland, Melissa Heatley moved in with Tiffany Evans, thereby continuing a relationship they'd begun five years earlier at school. Tiffany was nearly a year older than Melissa and not pretty in that her face was rather reminiscent of a very nice horse, but that never deterred her from being essentially stylish with an elegance that was all her own. She was also shrewd, out-going and from the age of thirteen had realised instinctively that Melissa needed a mentor, and been happy to be it. She came from a similar but at the same time rather different background to Melissa, in that she had wealthy parents too, but ones that had had an entirely different approach to bringing up children to the Heatleys. With the result that Tiffany was rather worldly-wise and had been for a long time.

She was also fun to be with and if Nanny Ellen and James Heatley had not been totally deceived by some of her more extravagant mannerisms and modes, they would have appreciated the sort of weather eye Tiffany kept over Melissa.

All the same it was through Tiffany that Melissa met Clayton Forrester.

But that didn't happen until several months after Melissa moved in with Tiffany. In the interim, Melissa got a job with an international airline because of her command of French and German, started a course in Japanese, an increasingly handy language to have some fluency in in the tourist trade, and was patently enjoying every moment of being free and independent with a sort of spontaneous delight that sometimes made Tiffany blink.

'You don't always want to look so eager about everything, Melissa,' Tiffany said once.

'Why not? I am.'

'I know. And it gives you away a little, you see.'

'How?' Melissa demanded.

Tiffany grimaced. 'It's hard to explain but I have to confess I feel some sympathy for your father. He must be living in daily dread of hearing that you've been gobbled up into the white slave trade, if there is such a thing, or that you've become the latest, lovely, fair, young addition to some impressionable sheik's harem, or that you've been conned into frittering away your inheritance to prove that the world is flat after all.'

Melissa grinned. 'I'm not as gullible as that, surely?' she replied. 'I know this might come as a surprise to you, and my father, but no-one has tried to put anything over me at all since I left home.'

Tiffany, who had a ruling passion for cats, stroked the Persian one in her lap and looked thoughtful. 'It's only been three months,' she murmured finally. 'But tell me how your love life is going? In the shape of Freddy White in particular, and also in general.'

'What love life?' Melissa queried looking vague, but she relented almost immediately with another grin. 'I'm having fun, Tiffany. That's how it's going. I like Freddy White even though he has damp palms and can't for long talk about anything that doesn't include Rugby Union—but he does take me to the *nicest* restaurants! And I like Barney McAllister even though he's crazy about cars and talks of very little else, doesn't think of much else for that matter—in fact I like all the eligible young men you've introduced me to. On my father's behalf, you've done a great job, Tiff! But I'm not in love with any of them,' she added as Tiffany looked rueful. 'Nor are they in love with me. We're simply . . . having a good time!'

'I should be relieved to hear that but somehow I'm not,' Tiffany commented. 'Even the most simple-minded, damp-palmed, sports-loving male has certain inherent thoughts on his mind.'

'I know that,' Melissa said airily. 'And I know how to handle it. Whenever they get that look in their eye, I start to tease them—nicely and not ever about their masculinity, that's hitting below the belt, but just a little gentle fun about their pre-occupation with Rugby and cars or whatever, and they retire hurt for a little while—men, if you can call great overgrown boys like Freddy White men—have egos about as strong as egg shells, had you noticed?'

'My God!' Tiffany said with some awe. 'Out of

the mouths of babes!' She shook her head. 'So you reckon you can handle them?'

'The Freddy Whites—sure! You see they're still feeling their way, they're preppys and they know it. Just as I know I am. And in the meantime we're having fun.'

'And have you never met anyone who wasn't in the preppy class?' Tiffany asked curiously.

'Oh yes,' Melissa said cheerfully. 'I had an awful crush on a ski instructor I had in Lausanne. He was lovely,' she said reminiscently. 'Just to look at him made my bones feel funny. They never do when I look at Freddy White. And when I got back to Glen Morris, there was a new farm manager who was just terrifyingly attractive, and nice too, but one day I saw him looking at me and somehow, I could see in his eyes, what he was thinking. What he'd like to do to me and although I'd indulged in some happy little day dreams about him, faced with reality, I found I was scared stiff! Which made me realise I had a bit of growing up to do before I got involved with any real men.'

'Well,' Tiffany stood up shovelling the indignant cat off her lap in the process, 'I guess you're more of a cautious Heatley than one would have imagined.'

'Are Heatleys cautious?'

'As a breed, very,' Tiffany said lightly. 'That's why they're so successful. By the way, in about a fortnight's time, you are invited to my parents annual shindig. Have I ever told you about it? They hold it once a year just for the sake of holding a party and everyone who is anyone is invited. Not that you fall into *that* category, they really would like you to come, and to bring Freddy or Barney or whoever is not retired hurt at the time.' She cast Melissa a teasing little smile. 'It's a formal, high fashion do too, so you can splurge on something stunning to wear. I am. I'm going to knock 'em cold this year.'

Whether she meant her parents in particular, or the world in general, Melissa wasn't sure. But in the spirit of not wanting to be outshone, Melissa took up the gauntlet over the matter of what to wear, with relish.

It took her over a week to find the perfect dress and when she did, it was so expensive, she had to break into the quarterly allowance her father insisted on making her—something she tried to avoid doing and had succeeded until now. But the dress took her breath away and she knew she couldn't resist it.

And when she was ready for the party, the reflection in the mirror effectively quelled her conscience.

Tiffany had spent the day at her parent's home, so Melissa had the flat to herself and much as she loved Tiffany, it was nice not to have to share the bathroom and be able to soak in the perfumed water and then dress leisurely to her own choice of music. This was one thing they didn't have in common, music. Tiffany was a great fan of pop music whereas Melissa loved classical.

She put on *The Nutcracker Suite* and closed her eyes and thought back to one of her rare visits to the Sydney Opera House as a child, to see the ballet. Then she started to dress.

It was red, this dream of a dress, and wildly sophisticated. A bright red that set off her very fair hair magnificently and made her fair skin look even fairer, like warm, creamy porcelain without blemish. It clung to her slender figure, highlighting her small high breasts without revealing, and the lovely curve of her hips and thighs. But its real impact came not from the glittering sequins it was embroidered with that made it glint in the light, but because it had one long, fitted sleeve but left her other arm and shoulder bare.

The only jewelry she wore was the diamond-studded bangle on her bare wrist that had been her eighteenth birthday present from her father, and her hair, which was smooth and straight and thick, was tonight curled and pulled into a bunch at one side to just brush her bare shoulder. High-heeled silver sandals completed the picture and the dress had come with a matching little drawstring bag, into which she pushed a comb, a hanky, a tube of the pale frosted lipstick she was wearing, and a twenty dollar note in the unlikely event that she should be stranded later without an escort. Nanny Ellen had made her promise she would always do this when she went out, but although Melissa kept that part of the promise faithfully, she didn't adhere to the rest of it strictly, for in Nanny Ellen's eyes no girl was equipped to face the world unless she went out at all times armed with a police-whistle, a long, deadly hatpin, saftey-pins, a needle and cotton for those things you couldn't pin up, a spare pair of tights, a manicure set—the list went on.

But as Melissa danced around the room to the lovely strains of Tchaikovsky's *Waltz of the Flowers*, she wasn't thinking of Ellen, she was admiring her dress, soaking up the music and feeling as light as a thistle.

Then the doorbell rang and she tripped over the Persian cat on her way to answer it, which reminded her she hadn't fed it as she'd promised.

Freddy stood at the door, looking nicer than she'd ever seen him, his tall, rather bulky figure suited to evening clothes, and his fair hair for once sleek. He carried a corsage of tiny cream orchids too, which surprised and delighted her and made her feel warmly fond of him. He was nice, you couldn't deny that and he'd been very well brought up— you couldn't deny that either. And he even offered to feed the cat while she pinned her corsage on. What she didn't notice though, was the slightly stunned look in his eyes when they first rested on her, which he normally reserved for a three-quarter-line goal, kicked through an acute angle.

And she went off to the Evans party with him, happy and bubbling with excitement and with not the slightest intimation that it was going to become at the same time the most important night of her life, and one with very drastic consequences.

To say that she took the party by storm wouldn't be quite accurate but it wasn't far off it. Even Tiffany, who was looking supremely elegant in lime green, gave her a salute in the form of a thumb and forefinger curled to make an O, indicating that Melissa was spot on—high praise from Tiffany.

And as the evening wore on and the beautiful, harbourside home hummed with music and gaiety, she was besieged by partners to dance with, to eat with, to drink with—in fact Freddy even grumbled once that he needed an axe to carve his way through her throng of admirers. But at about a quarter to midnight, she breathlessly grabbed his arm and begged him to find her a secluded spot where she could sit down for a while. He obliged and led her to a small table beside the pool and left her with a promise to be back with a long, cool, reviving drink.

Melissa sank down with a sigh and fanned herself with her hand and gave herself up to the exquisite beauty of the moonlight shining on the harbour, the faint smell of jasmine coming from a creeper nearby, and the headiness of her success.

Then a movement behind her intruded, and she turned to look upwards into a pair of wryly amused, light grey eyes. She hadn't heard anyone approach but this tall man with a drink in his hands was undoubtedly standing beside her, and what's more, she had the distinct feeling she was the object of his amusement.

'Hello,' she said uncertainly.

'Hello,' he responded. 'Has Cinderella come out here to await the pumpkin coach?'

'Why ... do you think that?' She stared up at him, taking in the clever lines of his face, the dark, thick hair which lay a little on his forehead and his long, square-tipped hands.

'Why?' A hint of a smile touched his lips. 'Because you're the belle of the ball—a mystery belle too, at least I imagine so from the number of people who've been asking who you are. That's why I thought of Cinderella when I saw you sitting here on your own.'

'Oh!' Melissa relaxed. 'There's no mystery about me. But it is the first time I've been to a party like this which is why people might not know me— have they really been asking about me?'

He pulled out a chair and sat down beside her. 'Yes they have,' he said gravely. 'At least three people have asked me about you.'

'I don't think I should believe you,' she said frankly.

'Why not?'

'Because I suspect you're teasing me. I think . . .' she put her head to one side consideringly, 'you're the kind of person who can tease with a perfectly straight face.'

He laughed. 'That's a very serious charge to lay,' he said gravely, but with his eyes still laughing at her. 'But no, I'm not teasing you. You've most certainly generated some interest tonight.' His eyes roamed over her, taking in the pure, lovely curve of her cheek, the straight little nose, and then moved fleetingly downwards. 'That's a fantastic dress,' he murmured, his eyes coming back to rest on her face.

Melissa flushed with pleasure, and something else she couldn't quite name, something his look had aroused that made her feel suddenly as if her heart was beating hurriedly and lightly and up near her throat. And hard on the heels of that sensation came a curious sense of inadequacy that was just as bewildering.

She said breathlessly, 'Thank you! I think so too although I virtually had to break the bank to buy it.'

A faint frown touched his brow. 'Then you're not the daughter of some noble family making her début?' he queried.

'Well . . .' She looked at him uncertainly.

'I thought so,' he drawled. 'There are only three kinds of people here tonight, the noble, the wealthy and the famous. Unless you're Cinderella after all?'

She pulled a face. 'No. But right as the moment I'm being perfectly independent of . . . my family. A least I was,' her cheek dimpled, 'until I fell in love with this dress!'

They laughed together for a moment. Then he said, 'Is that wise?'

'To want to be independent? I think so. They . . . sort of wanted to keep me under lock and key. Well, not exactly but,' she soloured faintly, 'they're very *nice*,' she added earnestly. 'Did you ever have that problem with your family?'

'Er . . . no. I think it's something very rich families reserve for their daughters,' he said apologetically. 'Besides, I don't have any close family left and anyway I'm a little old for it,' he added wryly.

'How old are you?' she asked and bit her lip. 'I don't mean to be rude . . .'

'That's all right,' he said perfectly seriously but with his eyes amused. 'I'm thirty-two. Quite old in fact, whereas you would be . . . eighteen?'

She grimaced. 'Nearly nineteen. I suppose to you that's awfully young. Are you,' she looked at him, 'I mean . . .' She trailed off awkwardly.

'Noble, wealthy or famous?' he murmured with his lips twitching. 'Only wealthy I'm afraid—the least interesting of the categories. Oh, it's enough to give one an entreé but . . .' He shrugged.

Melissa looked at him a little perturbed. 'I think it's silly to make distinctions like that. It's people who matter not . . . those other things.'

'Yes, ma'am,' he said meekly after a moment which didn't deceive her at all. But he relented suddenly, 'You're right. It's very silly. What else shall we talk about? By the way, have you been abandoned here?'

Melissa looked around and wrinkled her nose. 'I'm beginning to think I have! My date went to get a drink.'

'Have some of mine,' he offered. 'There's a

terrible crush around the bar. No, it's not alcoholic,' he said in response to the slightly wary look she cast the tall glass. 'It's plain old-fashioned lemonade. I was . . . er . . . unwise enough to indulge in a couple of glasses of the punch they were pressing on everyone as you stepped through the door—I should imagine it would make a good paint-stripper! And I decided in the interests of my head and my insides not to mix it with anything else alcoholic.'

Melissa grinned. 'I know what you mean. I had a glass too. It made my cheeks go concave. Thank you.' She accepted the glass from him and sipped it. 'Mmm, now that's nice.'

'Have it all then.'

'Do you mind?'

'No.'

'What's your name?' she asked.

'Clayton. What's yours?'

'Melissa. Really it's Melisande but for some reason my mother hated that . . .' She stopped and frowned as if this was a dredged-up fact she'd never really been aware of before. 'I don't know why,' she said slowly. 'But it's always been Melissa ever since I can remember.'

Her eyes focused on her companion and she frowned again because there was something suddenly taut in the way his long fingers had stopped fiddling with her little red bag on the table, and something narrowed and speculative and curiously alert in the way he was looking at her now—not at all with the wry amusement of several moments earlier.

'What is it?' she asked.

'Oh, nothing really,' he said after a brief pause. 'Just a coincidence.' He smiled slightly. 'My mother's name was Melisande.'

'Really? I've never met another one. Is she . . . but she's . . .' She trailed off awkwardly.

'Yes, she's dead,' he said quietly.

'I'm sorry.' Melissa said. 'My mother is dead too, so I know how you . . . can feel.'

He looked at her expressionlessly. Then something in his face softened and he said, 'Thank you, Melissa—or is it Melly? My father used to call my mother Sandy but I suppose in the case of Melissa . . .'

'Oh no!' Melissa looked stern. 'After that original change, no-one's ever been allowed to shorten my name. My father would have hated it and what he says goes! Besides,' her eyes danced, 'Melly Heatley doesn't sound . . . I don't know, quite mellifluous, don't you think?'

His grey eyes narrowed. 'Melly Heatley,' he said softly as if trying it for size. 'Melissa . . . Heatley.' He looked down briefly and when he looked up again his eyes were still narrowed but he was smiling. 'No, I like Melly,' he said, and at that moment Freddy arrived with two drinks.

'Oh *darn* it,' he said looking from Melissa to her companion. 'I've spent the whole night fighting my way through a crush to get to you, Melissa, and I've spent the last twenty minutes fighting my way through to the bar to get you a drink and now someone's taken my place!'

But the man called Clay pushed his chair back and stood up. 'Not at all,' he said with a grin. 'I've simply been . . . covering for you while you were away. Goodnight, Cinderella,' he said softly to Melissa but his eyes glinted with laughter. 'Look after her, Prince Charming,' he added to Freddy, and strolled away indoors.

'What did he mean?' Freddy asked. 'Melissa?'

Melissa turned to Freddy with a start. 'Nothing,' she said vaguely. Then, 'Do you know him, Freddy?'

Freddy shook his head. 'Don't think so. Why?'

But she only shrugged.

Yet the rest of the party seemed to have lost something, she discovered, although she danced into the small hours. And she found herself looking around from time to time for a pair of light grey eyes, but she didn't see them and concluded that the man who'd called her Cinderella had left early. Which, for some inconceivable reason, made her feel sad.

Not quite as sad, however, as when Freddy White tried to kiss her when he took her home. 'God, Melissa,' he said, 'you're so beautiful how can you expect me not to want to kiss you?'

'I . . .' she said helplessly. 'I thought we were just friends.'

But this hadn't been the right thing to say because he took himself off then, in furious disgust which was directed at her, and the Persian cat who tripped him up on the landing as he went. And Melissa was left with the not very pleasant feeling that between the two of them, herself and the cat, they'd managed to totally alienate him, which wasn't what she'd wanted to do.

So altogether, she reflected wearily as she got into bed, her first big party had turned into something of an anti-climax. But, apart from Freddy, it was hard to say why. Surely not just because of a man with clever grey eyes and a sometimes wickedly provocative smile . . .?

Surely yes, Melissa Forrester thought to herself as

she stared up at the ceiling of Tanya's spare room with bleak, pain-filled eyes. Because three days later, you were still thinking about him. Don't you remember how you asked Tiffany . . .?

CHAPTER THREE

'TIFF? Do you know anyone called Clayton?'

Tiffany spread her toast with marmalade and wrinkled her brow. 'Sounds like a drink,' she said. 'N-o-o. Do you?'

'Yes, no, I mean . . .'

Tiffany eyed her curiously. 'Go on,' she invited. 'Yes or no?'

Melissa pulled a face. 'I met someone called Clayton at your party. He . . . thought I was Cinderella—oh, only because . . .' She went on to explain what had happened.

'I see,' Tiffany said at last. 'And this strange man caught your imagination? I take it,' she added, 'he wasn't bald and fiftyish, with a paunch?'

Melissa coloured faintly then had to laugh. 'No, he's thirty-two—he told me that because I asked him—and he's tall, dark and . . .' She stopped and screwed up her eyes. 'And . . .'

'Devastating?' Tiffany looked at her enquiringly. 'I've met them too, you know. The kind that make your bones feel funny, quote unquote. But I didn't notice anyone *particularly* mouth-watering,' she said thoughtfully.

'Oh well,' Melissa shrugged. 'I just wondered.' She poured herself a cup of coffee and found herself hoping rather devoutly that Tiffany would dismiss the subject from her mind.

But the opposite occurred. Tiffany suddenly went rigid with a piece of toast half-way to her mouth and said in astonished accents. 'My God, Melissa, you don't mean Clayton Forrester?'

'I don't know . . .'

'Was it his first name?'

'I—well I think so.'

'Tall and dark?' Tiffany said rapidly, 'yes, you said that . . . with grey eyes?' Melissa nodded. 'The kind of man you'd sell your soul for?' Tiffany fired at her.

Melissa grinned ruefully. 'I don't know about that but . . .'

'Gorgeous,' Tiffany said with a sigh and bit into her toast. But she choked on it almost immediately. 'Melissa,' she said strongly when she'd got her breath back, 'honey, he's way out of your league, more, more so than the ski instructor or the farm manager. I wouldn't be surprised if he gobbles little girls like you up two at a time, so don't . . .'

'I'm not,' Melissa said with a tinge of impatience. 'I know he's way out of my league but I'd be surprised if he gobbled little girls up because he seemed really nice. And I think if you weren't— in his league as you put it—he just wouldn't be interested in you so you'd be quite safe.'

Tiffany chewed her lip. Then she said darkly, 'There's one league that you wouldn't be out of with most men, and that's sharing their beds. But I don't think he's precisely the *marrying* kind. That's what I meant. Because he's had plenty of opportunity—but look here, I'm intrigued. He was only at the party for a short time yet he seems to have spent most of it talking to you!'

'He spent twenty minutes talking to me, Tiffany. Then he surrendered me up to Freddy without a backward glance and I didn't see him again. Is that what you call gobbling up?' Melissa asked sweetly.

'No, but do I detect a slight note of pique in your voice?' Tiffany enquired.

'Well . . .' Melissa hesitated.

'Do I?'

'Oh—yes, just a little,' Melissa confessed with a grin. 'But go on, Tiff,' she begged, 'tell me about him before I die of curiosity.'

Tiffany sat back with another sigh. 'He's wildly wealthy for one thing. He's a . . .' she shook a hand in the air, 'a financial whizz-kid. Apparently when he was very young he was working for a private company that started to go broke but he persuaded the owner, an elderly man, to let him try to shake it out of the doldrums which he did so successfully, when the old man died, he left the company to Clay. The rest is legendary. He took over more companies with a similar history and did the same with them and now he's virtually a multi-national organisation in his own right. My father says he's one of the cleverest businessmen he knows as well as being the youngest and apparently he has a terrific reputation even,' Tiffany grimaced, 'with the old guard, despite his nouveau richness.'

Melissa thought for a bit. Then she said, 'Go on.'

'What were you thinking?' Tiffany asked curiously.

'Just that I had the feeling he was . . . clever. But go on, tell me more!'

'Well naturally, he's a wildly eligible bachelor,' Tiffany said with a grin. 'Yet a succession of the crème de le crème of the leading ladies of the land have not succeeded in trapping him into the fourth estate—in other words . . .'

'I know what that means,' Melissa murmured.

'Ah,' Tiffany said. 'Then you might understand too, for all the Cinderella bit, that even if he was a little attracted to you, and I'm not denying that's a possibility by any means, but even if he was there's no saying it would lead to matrimony. And that's a way a girl like you could get very hurt.'

'You mean a hick like me, don't you?' Melissa's cheek dimpled.

'I do not!' Tiffany looked shocked. 'A hick!'

'Well—naive, it's the same thing.'

'It is not!'

'It is to me.' Melissa smiled at her affectionately. 'I'm not offended! I just know what you mean. And I don't think we have anything to worry about because I'm sure he thinks the same! Particularly if you mean what I think you mean about the leading ladies of the land—you know, wildly sophisticated, probably clever too.'

'Well, Tiffany hesitated, 'yes. At least the ones I've known of were. *Known* of,' she emphasised, with a grimace. 'A little different from you and I. One was an airline executive, that kind of thing . . . the essence of chic and elegance and all in their mid to late twenties. You're probably right,' she said thoughtfully. 'He . . .'

But she didn't finish what she was about to say because the little dresser clock struck the hour musically then and they were both thrown into a mild state of panic to get to work on time. But if she'd been going to say that she didn't think Clayton Forrester would really be interested in Melissa, she was soon to be proved wrong—to Melissa's great surprise, despite the fact that all she'd learnt about him hadn't quite stopped her from thinking about him . . .

Two weeks after the party, Melissa left work at five o'clock adjusting her jaunty cap as she stepped out on to the pavement, and stopped dead. Because across the pavement from her a sleek grey sports car was parked in a loading zone and Clayton Forrester was leaning back against the roof with his arms folded.

Their eyes met and he straightened up. 'Cinderella,' he said lazily. 'You're right on time.'

Melissa's heart hammered uncomfortably and she turned pink. 'Are you—you're not waiting for me, are you?' she stammered.

'I don't know any other Cinderella,' he replied with a grin. 'I wondered if you'd like to have dinner with me?'

'I . . . why? I mean . . . how did you know where I worked, for starters?' she asked a little lamely.

He looked enigmatic. 'I have my sources. Do you have anything else on?'

'No. I . . . no. But why me?' Her lavender-blue gaze was suddenly troubled.

His lips quirked in a way she remembered. 'We never did get to finish our conversation,' he said wryly. 'Which is why I thought it might be a good idea to have dinner. And I very properly found out where you worked from Mrs Evans.'

'You could have rung me . . . up.'

His eyes glinted suddenly. 'And you can say no now, too.'

'I didn't mean that.'

'I'm glad. But you are hesitating.'

'I . . . didn't think I was your type.' Melissa closed her eyes briefly and cursed her honesty. When she opened them, it was to find him regarding her quizzically.

'Isn't it a little . . . silly,' he drawled finally, 'to

categorise people into "types" on the brief acquaintance we've had? After all, I might surprise you and you might surprise me. We might end up good friends, who knows?'

'Do you have . . . those kind of friends? I mean, lady friends?' she asked doubtfully.

'I . . .' He paused and looked at her very directly. 'I'm not in the habit of luring every passable female I meet into bed, if that's what you mean.'

A tide of bright colour flooded Melissa's cheeks and she bit her lip in an agony of embarrassment and confusion.

'That is what you thought,' he murmured as he scanned her hot, discomfited face.

'No,' she said. 'I didn't really. I thought you were nice only . . .' She stopped abruptly.

'Only—you've heard otherwise, perhaps,' he said a shade dryly.

'Yes—no! Not from anyone who really knows,' she said awkwardly. 'Just from someone who— knows me. I'm rather a hick, you see. Lately come to town you might say.' Her lips trembled into a rueful smile and her cheek dimpled. 'Everyone worries so much about me, you have no idea! So much so that I can't help realising I must be hopelessly unsophisticated and really wet behind the ears! Which is why,' she added with an imp of mischief dancing in her eyes, 'the idea of *you* wanting to take me to dinner, quite unnerved me,' she confessed. 'I'm sorry if I've been ungracious about it.'

The smile that had been growing at the back of Clayton Forrester's grey eyes as Melissa made her explanation, touched his lips and although he tried to prevent it, finally became a jolt of outright laughter. 'I don't know what to say to that,' he said, still grinning amusedly. 'The last thing I wanted to do was "unnerve" you. I only thought we might have dinner together because to be quite honest I found your brand of . . . unsophistication, rather refreshing and over the last week or two, I've thought it was a pity we were interrupted that night. And I promise I'll do nothing that even the most lately come to town girl, would take exception to. I—have a reputation for keeping my promises.'

'Well then,' Melissa smiled at him, totally disarmed, 'I'd love to!'

'Where would you like to go?' he asked when she was sitting beside him and he was easing the car through the peak hour traffic.

'I don't know.' She took her cap off and looked down at her uniform. 'I shouldn't really go out in this but if I take my badge off,' she unpinned it and obligingly the smart grey suit and fresh white blouse became less recognisable as a uniform, 'and if we go somewhere off the beaten track . . .'

'How about the Blue Mountains? There's a French restaurant at Katoomba where the food is excellent.'

'The Blue Mountains? That sounds terrific! Sometimes I long to get away from the city.'

'So be it,' he murmured and before long the powerful car was surging along the highway towards Penrith, and the Blue Mountains west of Sydney were living up to their name in the sunset.

'How's Prince Charming?' he asked idly as they drove through Penrith.

Melissa sighed. 'He's not talking to me. I'm afraid I really hurt his feelings this time.'

'Oh?' Clayton Forrester took his eyes off the road for a moment to let them rest on her profile.

'Yes.' She turned her head and smiled a little sadly.

'Would you like to tell me?'

She told him.

'You don't have to be kissed, if you don't want to be,' he said.

'I know.' She shrugged and looked down at her hands. 'But he did buy me a corsage and . . . well, I like Freddy. And I felt as if I'd led him on somehow but really, I don't—didn't think he felt that way about me. Not really.'

'Maybe that fantastic dress had something to do with it. I should imagine very young, impressionable men like Freddy might have looked at you that night, and wondered what had hit them on the head.'

She laughed a little breathlessly. 'If that's the case I better not ever wear it again!'

His eyes left the road again and met hers. 'That would be a pity,' he said lightly. 'I shouldn't worry too much. Very young men also have great powers of recovery.'

Their eyes held briefly and Melissa found she felt like pinching herself because she couldn't quite believe this was real.

And later that night in bed, she was conscious of the same feeling of unreality. Because hard as she tried to concentrate, curiously, she couldn't remember a great deal about the evening. Not in clear detail. She could remember that she had talked a lot and that Clayton Forrester had listened well and sometimes, often, with his eyes laughing at her. She could remember a superb *coq au vin* and a light, fruity Reisling and the clear mountain air. But she couldn't remember much of what she'd said and as she lay in bed, she wondered a little forlornly if she'd rambled *on* like an idiot. It hadn't felt like it at the time but . . .

One thing she did remember very clearly though was saying goodnight to him. He'd come upstairs with her to the flat door and for the first time in the evening, she'd found herself tongue-tied. Simply unable to think of a thing to say. And he'd looked down at her for a long moment before saying quietly, 'Thank you for a lovely evening, Melly. Do you mind if I call you that?' She shook her head. 'We must do it again sometime. Sleep well,' he'd added with a faint smile and a gentle pressure on her fingers and then he'd gone.

'I wonder if I'll ever see him again?' Melissa said into the darkness. 'Probably not unless we bump into each other. Oh why didn't I shut up and let him talk?'

She sighed, and a little later, fell asleep feeling unusually sad for the second time in as many weeks.

But over the next three months she saw quite a lot of him, and by design. Not that any of their meetings were prearranged from the last one, and sometimes a week or two elapsed before he would ring her up at the office and ask her if she was free that evening or sometimes, if it was a Friday, if she was free on Saturday or Sunday. So that she often wondered if she'd seen him for the last time unknowingly. But she never said anything about the uncertainty of it to him for several reasons. Throughout her life she'd been conditioned, in a sense, by her parent's frequent absences, to living a life of a sort of tempered expectancy. And she knew too how many demands there would be on his time if he was the kind of businessman her father was. Not that he ever discussed his work with her. But she knew all the same, when he casually mentioned things like having been in Paris last week, or Perth.

Then too, she said nothing because in her heart, she couldn't really understand why Clayton Forrester continued to want to see her. He'd been as good as his word and never done anything to upset or embarrass her—and seemed to have no idea of the things his mere presence did to her.

Another curious aspect of the whole thing was that she suspected that no-one who knew Clayton Forrester or Melissa Heatley, had any idea that they often dined together, or sailed on the harbour in his yacht, or sometimes hired horses to ride in the Domain, and quite frequently went to the zoo and the cinema together. For her part, it was, she had to admit, by design that none of her friends knew. She'd felt guilty about not telling Tiffany for a while, and yet been secretly pleased that Tiffany and Clay had contrived to miss each other on the odd occasions when he dropped her off at the flat. But she couldn't help wondering if he had his own design or people who he didn't want to know about *her*. In fact he never mentioned any friends or anyone to her, and she had not the slightest idea where he lived, or even where his office was.

She often thought about the strangeness of it all, and just as often tried not to think about her own feelings.

But there came a day when she could no longer hide from herself the fact that each meeting was getting harder for her for the simple reason that she was no longer content to be just a friend of his. That she couldn't stop herself from wondering what it would be like to feel his lips on hers, his long fingers on her skin, to see him laughing down at her as he often did, but lovingly too. That it was becoming a bitter-sweet torment to her to watch his tall body handling his yacht and to feel her heart beginning to thud painfully in her breast, and to wonder with horror, if he knew or would guess at her feelings.

And she began to feel ashamed of herself for the things she sometimes thought about in relation to Clayton Forrester, and indignant with herself for being such a fool because he so obviously didn't reciprocate those kind of feelings. At least, she didn't think he did but just sometimes, she wondered.

Like the time late one night when they'd been to see a film and were walking through a back street to his car, and she tripped on an uneven pavement block and would have fallen if he hadn't shot out a hand and grabbed her wrist, and pulled her to him.

'I'm all right,' she said breathlessly. 'Just clumsy,' she added ruefully and smiled up at him.

But his arms around her didn't immediately slacken and they stood like that for a minute or so and her smile faded and her eyes widened at the way he was looking down at her. And for one heart-stopping moment she thought he was going to kiss her and her lips trembled and her body seemed to melt against him. But at the same time there was something frightening about it, about the intensity of what she felt, which might have shown in her eyes because his gaze narrowed and she felt his hands move on her back just gently,

and he put her away from him, and said
'The last thing I would accuse you of is being clumsy. It's this darned pavement. Here, hold my hand.'

And when her jumbled senses had calmed down a bit, she thought she must have imagined it—that he'd been going to kiss her—and she had felt like crying.

The other occasions that had given her cause to wonder had been even less spectacular. Things as trivial as looking up and finding him watching her when she hadn't expected it. And feeling herself flushing and hoping to God she was only imagining that feeling of heat in her cheeks, and leaping into the breach with something silly to say.

Perhaps he thinks of me as the sister he never had, she thought confusedly once. Would that explain why he keeps seeing me?

Another aspect of it that puzzled her was that it was all so ordinary, what they did, what they said to each other and sometimes she felt like pinching herself because after all this was Clayton Forrester who was not only wildly clever and successful, but wildly sophisticated by all accounts. Yet going to the cinema, riding, sailing, going to the zoo were not exactly sophisticated pursuits.

Not that he ever once looked or sounded bored but she couldn't help knowing that the tiny corner of his life that was apparently reserved for Melissa Heatley must be very different from the rest of it. And not that it inhibited her a great deal she found. She might get her emotions into a tangle over him but she never ran out of things to say, although they were such ordinary kinds of things she had to confess. Like how much she was enjoying a certain television series, or the book she was reading . . . a host of trivia in fact, except for the odd really deep discussions they got into.

And by the time she'd known him for three months there was very little she hadn't told him about her life from her early childhood to her teens, her experiences at school and in Switzerland, her passionate likes and dislikes, her love for Glen Morris and even, that when she got over excited she had an awful tendency to get sick, a thing she'd done religiously once a year at the Yass Show. Although lately she really thought she'd conquered it.

In return she didn't learn nearly as much. For one thing it seemed that there was some sort of an embargo on talking about *his* childhood. He simply clammed up when she asked any questions and she came to the conclusion that it must have been rather an unhappy one. She thought too that it might account for a certain hardness she sometimes fleetingly saw in him.

But she did come to know a lot of little things about him, that he'd already read every author she mentioned, that he was the only person she knew who regularly got *The Times* crossword out, that he had very widely ranging tastes in music, in fact he told her once that one of his favourites was the theme music to *Doctor Who*, that he was something of a workaholic, that he loved oysters . . .

Nothing earth-shattering, but worse, she sometimes thought, *nothing* that gives me one clue as to why he keeps on seeing me. Has he run out of crème de la crème ladies? But I can't believe that . . . I wonder if he has the same effect on them as he has on me? And I wonder if he teases them sometimes like he teases me?

'And I wonder,' she murmured to herself once, 'what they do when just to look at him makes them tremble inwardly and feel hot and cold at the same time? Do they let him know in some subtle way? Or do they just come out and say it? Which I could never do . . .'

So it was with very mixed feelings that she continued to see Clayton Forrester. Added to this was the circumstance of Freddy. For quite a while after the party whenever their paths had crossed unwittingly, which was hard to avoid as they had a lot of mutual friends, he'd looked at her with a cold sort of resentment and metaphorically speaking, turned his back on her. Then things changed and she began to find that whenever they were part of the same crowd, very often when she looked up it would be to find his eyes on her and the burning intensity she saw in them before he looked away, sent a cold little chill down her spine.

He's not really still smarting about that night, she told herself several times. Nor is he really in love with me. He just thinks he is like I . . . think I'm in love with Clay . . .

But this thought chilled her as much as Freddy White's burning looks until she shook herself. At least I don't go about looking cross and . . . oh damn! I just won't think about any of it any more!

But despite this, and her instinctive resolution never to be caught alone with Freddy, it happened one evening that he found her home on her own. And there followed an uncomfortable interlude for both of them. He tried to profess his undying love for her and when she tried to tell him it was at most a passing fancy, he got angry and grabbed her and kissed her wetly and with all the strength he was capable of, which was considerable—he was six foot two and well suited, body-wise, to the position of forward which he played with such verve.

At first Melissa was angry as she tried desperately to struggle free, then she became frightened and curiously numb and she made a small choked sound in her throat and it was that that made him release her, to stare down at her white, frightened face and huge, darkened eyes for a long moment.

'Oh God,' he said thickly then and closed his eyes. 'I'm sorry!' And an expression of supreme self-disgust crossed his face. 'I'm sorry,' he said hoarsely again.

Melissa tried to speak. 'Th-that's all right . . .'

'No it isn't,' he said. 'You must really hate me now!'

'I never hated you, Freddy. I just . . .'

'Don't love me,' he finished for her. 'But that doesn't change how *I* feel, Melissa. I'll love you until the day I die! I'll *never* love anyone else like this.' And with those dramatic words, he turned on his heel and left.

Melissa lifted a hand and touched her lips which felt strange, and for a while wasn't sure whether she wanted to laugh or cry.

She still wasn't sure the next day whether she should be angry or feel a haunting sort of compassion for Freddy White, and then Clay rang and asked her to go sailing with him the following day which was Saturday.

'I . . . I . . .' she stammered into the phone.

'What is it?' his cool, clipped tones came down the wire.

'Nothing! I . . . yes thanks, I'd like to. Shall I bring something to eat?'

'We could buy something.'

'Oh no, I don't mind cooking a chicken and . . . but it's up to you.'

There was a pause, then he said, 'I like the way you cook chicken. I'll bring a bottle of wine . . .'

The Bali Hai was a sleek, fast, racing yacht easily enough handled by two people, and increasingly Melissa was coming to know more about sailing. That Saturday there was a playful breeze on the harbour and they tacked back and forth for a couple of hours then found a secluded, protected cove and pulled the boat up on to the beach. She unpacked the picnic basket she'd brought while Clay rigged up a spare sail for shade. And they ate the cold chicken and salad she'd prepared with their fingers, and left greasy finger marks on the wine glasses he'd brought.

'You're quiet today, Melly,' he said as he poured some more wine into their glasses. 'Is something wrong?'

Melissa stared out over the sunlit, dancing water and didn't answer immediately. It was very peaceful, with only the sound of wavelets breaking gently against the shore and some birdsong from the trees behind the beach to disturb the silence.

'Am I?' she said at last and glinted a wry smile at him. 'That must be a change for you. I always talk myself silly when we get together. Oh! Look what I found at the greengrocer's this morning.' She reached over to the lunch basket. 'These two beautiful, absolutely mouthwatering-looking pears.' She lifted the succulent, speckled-yellow pears that were faintly flushed with pink, from their wrapping and offered him one. 'Try it.'

He took one from her but didn't look at it.

Instead, his grey gaze played over her thoughtfully and she found herself trapped by it, unable to look away.

Clay always wore the same outfit when they went sailing, dark blue board shorts and a white T-shirt that highlighted his tan. His shorts were multi-purpose—he swam in them too, and this casual outfit, she'd found, made him look younger and just sometimes, she could imagine he wasn't who he was, a wealthy business magnate, when he was wearing it. It was hard to forget that when he took her out to dinner dressed in a conservative suit. But staring at him now, with his long legs bare and his hair ruffled and his body relaxed, sprawled on the blanket they'd spread, and half-raised on one elbow, he seemed nearer her level somehow, not so unattainable—only he wasn't of course, she thought, and looked away suddenly. It's only my imagination . . .

'I gather you don't want to talk about what's upset you, Melly,' he said finally.

'No—there's nothing, really.' She jumped up and pulled off her T-shirt, completely revealing her one-piece coral-pink bathing suit. 'It think I'll have a swim. Coming?'

But he shook his head and bit into his pear.

She frolicked in the water for about fifteen minutes and when she came out, he was sitting up, cross-legged, and he handed her a towel and then her glass of wine.

'The water's lovely,' she said as she sipped her wine and dried her hair perfunctorily with her other hand. 'You should have come in!' She smiled at him and sat down. 'Now I'll have my pear! Could you pass it to me?' She held out her hand but frowned immediately. 'What is it? Why are you looking at me like that?' Her hand dropped uncertainly.

'You're bruised,' he said slowly and leant across the intervening space to touch her arm. 'Turn round.'

She did after a slight hesitation and he fingered her other arm. She turned back to look at him enquiringly. 'What is it?'

'You have two sets of perfect finger marks on your upper arms. No, you probably won't be able to see them,' he said as she tried to peer awkwardly at the backs of her arms. He tilted her chin up with one hand. 'Have you acquired a ... savage lover, Melly?' he asked. 'Is that what you don't want to tell me?'

Melissa blushed and tried to move her head but he didn't release her chin and his eyes probed hers.

'No ... I ... oh!' she said disjointedly. 'It must have been Freddy. But he didn't mean to do it. He just got carried away—he was absolutely horrified afterwards! And I feel terribly, horribly guilty. He said he would *never* love anyone else. I don't know what to do ...'

'What did he do to you?' Clay released her chin.

'He ... grabbed me and kissed me. For weeks he looked at me as if he *hated* me then, he looked different but ...' She sighed suddenly. 'But he's nice really, you know,' she said. 'I just think he ... well, I told you how he tripped over the cat? I think that was a tremendous blow to his ... dignity, on top of me rejecting him, so it's all sort of blown up out of proportion ... you're laughing,' she said miserably as Clay's lips twitched. 'How could you? I suppose you're so super cool about these things you never trip and you never think you're in love when you're not, and I suppose you know just how to handle someone who might think they were in love with you when you didn't want them to be.' Her voice was stiff with reproach and she blinked away a tear.

'I don't think it's a question of being super cool,' he said gravely, 'merely quite a bit older.' He watched her unhappy countenance in silence for a bit. Then he said, 'Apart from those bruises, did he hurt you?'

She considered and involuntarily, one hand crept up to her lips. 'No,' she said finally. 'I got a fright more than anything else. It was like trying to fight off a bear. But I think he's turned me off kissing.' She looked rueful.

Clayton Forrester reached out a hand and fiddled with a strand of her hair. 'Poor Melly,' he said on a strange note. 'That would be a pity. Hasn't anyone else kissed you?'

'No. I mean, not a man.'

'Perhaps I could rectify that,' he murmured and her eyes flew to his and widened. 'Oh, in the interests of not having you turned off it for life,' he added.

Melissa tried to speak but found she couldn't. Nor did she move as he slid his arms around her and gathered her closer, although her heart began to beat slowly and heavily.

'This won't hurt,' he said softly and smiled slightly at her bemused expression. 'And anytime you don't like it, I'll stop, I promise.'

He bent his head then and when his lips touched hers, they didn't feel in the least like Freddy White's, but were cool and firm, and she closed her eyes after a moment and felt her body begin to relax and her mouth tremble beneath his.

Clayton Forrester took his time about kissing Melissa Heatley for the first time. As if he had all the time in the world. Indeed, for Melissa, it felt as if the world had stopped. Nor, she realised dimly, did any of her daydreams about Clay kissing her bear much relation to the reality of it. She hadn't known for instance that the feel of his lips on hers would cause her whole body to come alive with an urgent sense of need, cause her skin to shiver of its own accord and tingle, and a curious sensation at the pit of her stomach to grow. Or that she would feel so slender in his arms, and want to run her hands across his shoulders and press her fingers through his hair, and mould the vibrant slenderness of herself to the long hard planes of his body and feel enveloped, crushed, as one with him.

And when it finished, she lay breathless and shaken with her forehead resting on his shoulder, not knowing what to say or do and after a minute or so, conscious of a growing, terrible sense of desolation because she knew this would be the first and only time he would ever kiss her.

'Melly?' he said gently after what seemed like an everlasting, soul-destroying age. He put a hand to the back of her head and stroked her hair.

She took a deep breath and made herself speak although her throat hurt with unshed tears. 'Thank you,' she said in muffled tones and lifted her head at last to smile crookedly at him and pray at the same time that none of what she was feeling would show in any way. 'That was . . . that was . . . much better.'

His grey eyes narrowed and his hand left her hair to trace the outline of her mouth just once. 'Thank *you*,' he said slowly. 'You're very lovely, did you know? I'm not really surprised that the

Freddy's of this world ... lose their cool about you. Tell me,' he added abruptly and put her gently away from him, 'doesn't your father ... I mean, wouldn't you be better off living with him or with a ...' He hesitated.

'A chaperone? That's what he wanted. And he keeps tabs on me,' she laughed, 'even when he's overseas his secretary rings me twice a week. But I thought it was time I became a bit independent. After all I'm nineteen now, really nineteen.'

'And ... what will you do the next time Freddy White tries to kiss you, Miss Really Nineteen?' he asked with just a touch of irony.

'I ...' Melissa's cheek dimpled, 'I might just tell him to go out and get lessons before he tries it on me again now that I know ... that ...' her voice faltered and her impish smile faded a bit but she pinned it back determinedly, 'now that I've had some.'

'He might find that as humiliating as tripping over the cat,' Clay said wryly. 'Why ...?'

But she didn't let him finish because the hurt in her heart was growing if anything, spurred on by this conversation that demonstrated quite clearly that Clay thought she was young and probably silly too, and unable to take care of herself. Why did he bother to kiss me, she wondered mutinously, if he thinks I need a chaperone?

'Let's forget about Freddy,' she said determinedly. 'I have! It's much too nice a day to be bothered about things like that. Are we going to laze here forever?' she teased.

He regarded her thoughtfully for a moment and her poor heart which had suffered so much in such a short time, felt as if it was being squeezed in her breast just because of the way his hair was lying on his forehead—I can't take much more of this, the thought flashed across her mind. Please God just let me get through the rest of this day . . .

'All right.' He grinned at her suddenly. 'You pack up and I'll get the boat in the water, and seeing as you're feeling so energetic, you can sail her. I'll just sit back and give orders.'

'Oh could I?' Her eyes shone and no-one watching her would have known what a supreme act she was putting on, as if she had not another thought on her mind. 'What if I capsize us?'

'You'll just have to be happy that I'll be there to right us,' he drawled and stood up in one lithe movement that did further queer things to her heart. But not as queer as what he did next. He leant down a hand and pulled her to her feet and kissed her lightly on her forehead. 'But you're not going to capsize us, are you, Melly?' he drawled. 'Not after all I've taught you!' he threatened with mock severity.

'No, Clay,' she answered. 'I won't forget a thing you've taught me . . .'

But I did, Melissa Forrester told herself nearly three years later. I . . . although at the time, for a while, it felt as if I was trying to tear out my heart. And I kept telling myself that if I'd had any sense, I'd have never let you teach me anything else, Clay. Then I wouldn't have had so much to forget, to . . . unlearn. But I did it.

And at the time, I couldn't understand how I could have been so stupid, how I'd missed all the signs—I still don't really . . .

'Although I must have had some subconscious presentiment,' she murmured and moved her wheat-fair head on Tanya Miller's sapphire-blue pillow slip. 'That's why, after the day we went sailing and he kissed me, I decided that night not to see him anymore. If only I'd stuck to that decision ... But he came to see me, after I'd declined an invitation to go out with him, which Tiffany overheard me doing. I'd forgotten she was sitting at the kitchen table when he rang ...

CHAPTER FOUR

'I CAN'T, Clay,' Melissa said awkwardly into the phone. 'I . . .' She turned round suddenly and as she'd remembered too late, Tiffany was sitting at the kitchen table but with her mouth hanging open now. Melissa turned back to the phone. 'I'm sorry but I'm booked up for ages. Thank you for thinking of me though.' She hesitated and bit her lip. 'See you sometime,' she said, and put down the phone.

'Melissa, is that who I think it was?'

'Probably,' Melissa said wearily.

'You dark horse! Or is that the first time he's . . . but it isn't, is it?' Tiffany said slowly and slapped her palm against the side of her head. 'That's who the mystery man has been! The dates you've been so cagey about! Why, oh why, didn't it dawn on me?'

'I don't know. It was your mother who told him where I worked,' Melissa said a shade wryly.

'She did? She never told me he was enquiring after you. But then's she's got a memory like a colander, I always knew that. So . . . now you're giving him the brush off?'

Melissa grimaced. 'It's not like that.'

'It sounded like it to me,' Tiffany said wisely and stopped as she was about to say something else. 'When did you last see him?' she enquired finally.

Melissa shrugged and tried to look off-hand. 'Three weeks ago. We . . . went sailing.'

'And for the last three weeks you've been looking the picture of misery. Want to tell me why?'

'I haven't been looking a picture of misery,' Melissa denied. 'Oh, leave it will you, Tiff. I don't want to talk about it.'

'That's all very well,' Tiffany said militantly, 'but *I* do! What has he done to you? Has he been stringing you along, because . . .'

'He's done *nothing*, Tiffany,' Melissa said flatly. 'Absolutely nothing. He's treated me like his favourite niece or his kid sister.'

'Then . . . oh,' Tiffany said softly. 'I see. And you never got over your . . . Cinderella fantasies, is that it, Melissa?'

Melissa shut her eyes and for once in her life wished her best friend somewhere else, preferably on the other side of the moon. She sighed slightly. 'Something like that.' She shrugged.

Tiffany frowned. 'Then you've done the right thing, kid,' she said briskly. 'You should never have . . . but all the same . . . I wonder why he spent so much time with you if . . .' She didn't finish.

'I wondered that too,' Melissa said. 'I think he just liked me—as a friend. It can happen, can't it?' She pulled out a chair and sat down. 'Maybe I should have been content with that,' she said more to herself. 'I wish I could have. I feel as if there's a great big hole in my life now, you see. And if you must know, I'm sorry now that I did what I just did.'

'Hmmm,' Tiffany said judiciously. 'I still think it's for the best if you'll forgive me for saying so. And so will you soon,' she said bracingly. 'I wish you'd told me you know, though. After all, I'm supposed to be keeping an eye on you. And here you are, going out and about with the most divine man behind my back. I tell you, I feel . . . I can't help feeling a little piqued!'

They eyed each other and then both burst out laughing. 'That's better,' Tiffany said gently a little later. 'Honey, believe me, I think we've both got a fair way to go before we worry too much about the likes of Clayton Forrester. Did you ever meet Carmen Beresford?'

'No. Who's she?'

'She was his mistress. They broke up about six months ago—no, you wouldn't have met her because she went overseas straight afterwards. She was, let's see—she'd be about twenty-seven and she was just the last word in elegance, chic, wit . . . everything to make the likes of you and me go home and gnash our teeth and realise we're still novices.'

'He said . . . he found that refreshing.' Melissa bit her lip as soon as the words were out.

'Well, sure. But he didn't do anything about it, did he?'

'He . . . kissed me once.'

'I thought you said . . .'

'Oh, it wasn't like that. It . . . was nothing like that.' She stood up rather clumsily. 'You're right, Tiff.' She deliberately injected her voice with a false bravado. 'There was only one thing to do and now I've done it. End of verse and chapter. What shall we have for dinner? How about . . . Welsh Rarebit à la Melissa? You'll like it, I promise you, I have this secret recipe,' she added as Tiffany pulled a face.

'All right, seeing as how I'm broke and you're broke . . . uh-huh . . . in a very temporary sense of the word, I'll risk it. You're very domesticated, you know, Melissa,' she said curiously.

'I should be. I was educated to be at the cost of a small fortune, no doubt. We had a Cordon Bleu Chef to teach us to cook, a world-renowned interior decorator to tell us how to refurbish our stately homes, a Paris designer to tell us about clothes ... I really should be.'

'Now that's what I call strange,' Tiffany said. 'It's not as if you're ever going to *make* your clothes or personally re-decorate Glen Morris or cook your meals once you're established. Do these finishing schools work on the premise that hard times can befall the richest of us?'

Melissa shivered suddenly for no real reason. 'I'm sure it can happen,' she said and laughed a little because at least Tiffany's mind had been seemingly disengaged from Clayton Forrester.

If only I could get him out of my mind, she thought several days later.

It was about eight o'clock and a wet, rather dismal Friday evening with an autumnal chill in the air. So much so that Melissa had dug out her winter dressing gown nd changed into it and pyjamas after a warm bath. It was also a depressing kind of evening, mainly because she'd turned down two invitations to go out and now regretted it. Tiffany had gone home for the weekend and Melissa wished briefly that she could do the same—at least, go and spend the weekend with her father but he'd left for overseas two weeks earlier.

'I should have gone home to Glen Morris,' she told herself as she sat down at the kitchen table which did duty for a dining-room table and a host of other things in the small flat. 'I will next weekend when Tiffany's home to feed her cat!' she vowed. 'It's months since I've been home.'

And feeling a little heartened, she turned to her Japanese books and prepared to concentrate.

But the doorbell rang almost immediately and she went to open the door with a small frown. To find Clayton Forrester standing on the doorstep.

She gasped and went pink and spluttered incomprehensibly—all of which brought a faint, cool smile to his lips before he said, 'May I come in? Or are you going to bed?'

'No! I mean ... I was cold, that's all.' She looked down at her violet-blue, velvet dressing gown with something like despair and swallowed. 'Yes, if you'd like to. I was sitting in the kitchen,' she went on breathlessly as he followed her into the flat. 'It's warmer in there but we can ...'

'The kitchen will do fine,' he said.

'Oh. Well, come in. Sit down,' she invited and moved her books aside.

He pulled out a chair and sat down with his long legs sprawled out in front of him. And immediately, the bright homely kitchen shrank. Melissa stared at him for a moment as he looked around. He was conservatively dressed in a grey suit and a plain white shirt with a matching grey waistcoat—as if he'd just come from a board meeting, which he probably has, she thought. There were lines of weariness beside his mouth that she noticed because they weren't usually there, at least not when they went sailing or to the zoo. Oh God! she thought, why has he come?

She followed his gaze around the room, saw it rest on her African Violet which was flowering with a waxy, pale-purple, gay abandon for no reason that she could discern seeing it was the first time it had flowered for months; and rest briefly on the large crazy calender that was Tiffany's and then on the notes stuck all over the fridge door with small, brightly coloured, fish-shaped magnets that said, each one of them in capital letters—DON'T FORGET TO FEED MY CAT!!! And she saw his eyebrows lift.

'He always acts as if I've starved him whenever Tiffany's been away,' she said hastily. 'That's why she leaves me notes. He really is an impossible cat!'

'He would seem to be.'

'W-would you like a cup of coffee? I was just going to make one.' She didn't wait for an answer, just turned away to plug in the kettle and turned back almost immediately. 'Or would you like something stronger? We still have half a bottle of Tia Maria left over from our last party.'

'Why don't we have them both? They go well together, coffee and Tia Maria.'

'Of course! I should have thought of that.'

It took her about five minutes to make the instant coffee and pour the Tia Maria. Five dead quiet and totally nerve-racking minutes during which she fumbled and fiddled around and finally produced the goods. Five minutes which felt like fifty.

'Cheers,' she said and raised her liqueur glass. 'Did you come to see me about anything in particular?'

He looked at her steadily, his grey eyes narrowed and curiously sombre. 'Yes I did,' he said at last. 'I came because I got the feeling we didn't part the best of friends, Melly. And I found that disturbing.'

'Well, there's no reason for us not to be friends,' she said cautiously, 'that I know of.'

'There's every reason,' he said.

She stirred her coffee in a frightened kind of silence.

'Melly?'

She lifted her eyes to his at last.

'At least there's the good reason,' he said, 'that for no apparent reason, you don't want to be friends anymore.' His eyes flicked over and came back to rest on her face. 'Was it because I kissed you?' he asked with a total lack of emotion.

She coloured brilliantly and immediately realised how she'd given herself away with that one burning tide of red in her cheeks. So that there seemed to be only one thing to say. Which she said briefly. 'Yes.'

'Shouldn't I have done it?' he asked. 'It,' he hesitated and his eyes probed her hot face, 'it was a spur of the moment thing. You reminded me of a ... bruised flower and you seemed to be so confused about Freddy and—those things in general, I rather acted on impulse you might say. I'm sorry if I offended you.'

Melissa moved restlessly and found that her hands seemed to have a life of their own which made them fiddle with her Japanese books, then her coffee cup and finally her glass until she spilt a little of the Tia Maria. She put her finger on the brown spot of liquid and lifted it to her mouth and licked it. Then she sighed suddenly and looked directly at him.

'You didn't,' she said gruffly. 'I wasn't upset that you kissed me. I was upset because from the first time I met you, I couldn't help wondering what it would be like ... if you kissed me. For three months I've been wanting you to—I know that sounds awful but it's true. And for three months now, I've known that that wasn't how you thought of me but I've,' she grimaced, 'well, that's how I've thought of you. Oh!' she said concernedly, 'you mustn't feel too embarrassed. I've felt this way before about—about men who didn't, well, I had a sort of crush on them. But it's always passed. Only this time it's taking longer to pass.' She swallowed and managed to smile ruefully. 'That's why I decided it would be best not to see you again, though, and I hope you don't mind me telling the truth, silly as it might sound, but I'd rather you didn't think I was being ... I didn't ... oh damn,' she said helplessly, 'I don't think I should have said any of that! Because now you might think ...'

'Melly,' he interrupted with a curious little smile playing on his lips, 'can I tell you something?'

'What?' she asked uncertainly.

'For the last three months I've been prey to the same emotions. In fact the very first time I laid eyes on you—not quite the first time—but certainly when I came upon you sitting in the moonlight, which was not so long after I first saw you, I thought you were the most exquisite, fresh, lovely young thing I'd ever seen and if Freddy hadn't turned up, I'm sure I'd have thought of a plan to lure you away because I was very conscious of the fact that I'd like to be able to hold you in my arms and kiss you breathless.'

Melissa's lips parted with a sort of stunned surprise. 'You're not serious?' she whispered at last.

He looked at her with a kind of wry irony. 'I'm

afraid so. Why do you think I sought you out again? Why do you think I'm here now?'

'I . . . I . . .' she stammered. 'But you've never . . . showed it . . .'

'Perhaps that's because you didn't know what to look for,' he said just a little dryly. 'Then too, I made you a promise if you recall. I told you I wouldn't do anything to upset you. I meant to stick to that promise until I felt, really felt you were ready. And I haven't been quite honest with you, Melly. I did think you were ready that last day—there seemed to be something about you that told me that you wouldn't very much mind if I kissed you. But I have to confess as well, that once I saw those bruises, I would have done so anyway because the thought of you being mauled and frightened was a little more than I could stand.'

'Oh Clay,' she whispered, and stared into his eyes. 'I think I must be dreaming.'

'If you come here, I'll show you that you're not.'

She did. A little hesitantly at first but by the time they were ensconced far more comfortably on the settee in the lounge, she'd lost a lot of her hesitancy.

In fact, it took the Persian cat to bring her back to reality.

'You're right about that damned cat,' Clay said against the corner of her mouth, and ran his fingers through her hair. 'It's a monster! No wonder Freddy got into such a state. Haven't you fed it?'

'Yes! It's had double rations tonight. It doesn't like to think it's not the centre of attraction, you see. It's a very *vain* cat to make matters worse.'

He laughed softly and kissed the lovely line of her throat so that she shivered with pleasure. 'Well if it thinks it's going to become the star attraction or that it can sit there and yowl at us, it's mistaken. Besides which ... maybe we need a timely interruption,' he murmured and moved her out of his arms to lay her back against the corner of the settee and pull a cushion up to rest behind her head.

'What are you going to do?'

'Deal with it,' he said mildly, and stood up. The cat immediately sprang up into the space he'd vacated but he scooped it up with one hand, taking it so much by surprise that it didn't protest until they were both in the kitchen where he cunningly diverted its attention anyway by opening the fridge door.

From the sounds she heard then, Melissa guessed that he was pouring it a saucer of milk. And two minutes later, he re-appeared with two glasses of Tia Maria in one hand and he shut the kitchen door firmly with the other.

'It will start to yowl again,' she said with a grin, 'as soon as it realises it's shut in.'

He handed her a glass. 'We'll see.' He sat down again but not close to her, in fact in the other corner of the settee with one arm laid across the back of it. 'Cheers,' he said. 'Melly ...'

'I know what you're going to say.'

He raised one eyebrow. 'Do you?'

'Yes.' She twirled her glass in her fingers for a moment then lifted her lavender blue gaze to his. 'That we should stop and think and thereby ... maybe save our souls from sin.' The old-fashioned phrase was one that Nanny Ellen had used frequently and Melissa closed her eyes exasperatedly as soon as the words left her lips. 'I don't know why I said that! It's not quite what I meant.'

Her eyes flew open as she heard him laugh softly, and she had to smile ruefully back. 'I say some stupid things sometimes.'

'As a matter of fact, you hit the nail on the head then.' he observed with a glint of laughter still in his eyes. 'Not that we've done anything sinful yet.'

She took a breath and looked at him with a sudden wariness in her eyes that she couldn't prevent.

'Melly,' he said softly, 'do you have any reservations about what generally follows when two people feel about each other the way we do?'

'I . . .' She hesitated. 'Well, in the context of sin, it doesn't seem to be such a sinful thing to do these days. I mean everybody does it—almost everybody. At least three of the girls I work with are living with their boyfriends. That's three out of four—three out of five if you include me, but it's still a high proportion. And Tiffany always says when the right bloke comes along she'll go to bed with him first and then . . .' She shrugged.

He regarded her silently but his eyes were amused. Then he said, 'Is that what you'd like us to do? Live together?'

'I . . . didn't say that,' she answered awkwardly but managed to glint a tiny, wry grin at him. 'Anyway you haven't asked me. But it is what a lot of people do when they . . . when they feel this way,' she finished, her voice very low.

'I had something else in mind,' he said after a moment. 'Something less fashionable but something that would suit *you* better, I think. Getting married.'

She went white and for the second time that night spilt some Tia Maria only this time the whole, though blessedly small, glassful. But it was enough to make a brown puddle on the lap of her velvet dressing gown before it soaked in. Not that she was aware of what she'd done although Clay noticed it and when his eyes came back to rest on her pale face, there was a tinge of irony in them and something like self-mockery that twisted his lips briefly. But she saw it and thought it was directed at her so that she went as red as she'd been white and bent her head, to notice for the first time, the stain on her lap.

She sprang up then, in a fever of agitation and feeling about as foolish as it was possible to feel and the liqueur glass slipped out of her fingers and rolled across the carpet. Shades of Freddy, she thought incoherently. I know now how he must have felt!

But Clay was on his feet too, a split second after she'd jumped up and he put a hand on her shoulder and wouldn't let her pull away.

'Melly,' he said on a laughing breath, 'what's wrong? Getting married is a time honoured way of doing things for all that it might be slightly out of vogue these days.'

'But . . .' She turned to him convulsively and then found she couldn't go on.

'But what?' he asked with his lips barely moving. 'Don't you want to marry me?'

'That's not the point . . .'

'Let's take one thing at a time. Do you or don't you?' His eyes probed hers and she noticed, strangely, that he was paler than normal suddenly, and that the lines of weariness beside his mouth were back.

She couldn't help herself. She lifted a hand to touch those lines with her fingertips, and made a queer little sound in her throat. 'Yes I do but . . .'

He captured her fingers in a strong grip. 'So many buts,' he murmured. 'But when you thought of me like this,' he touched his lips to the palm of her hand, 'as you said you did, what did you think you'd do about it if we discovered we *both* felt this way?'

She stared up at him and felt her heart jolt.

'Melly?' he prompted.

'I . . .' she whispered, 'I dreamt about us getting married. But don't you see, Clay, those were *daydreams*. And I—I told you I was a hick, didn't I? Well those are the kind of daydreams hicks like me have.' She tried to smile but it didn't come off very well. So she took a deep breath. 'What I'm trying to say is, I don't suppose you've asked everyone you've felt this way about, to marry you, and I don't want you to feel you have to ask me to marry you because . . . to save my soul from sin, because I'm . . . a bit more naive than most, probably.'

He pulled her right into his arms and his eyes were bright and strangely enigmatic as they roamed her confused, troubled face. 'The thing is,' he said almost wryly, 'I've never *felt* about anyone quite the way I feel about you. I miss you when you're not around, and I worry about you. I also know you well enough to know that you're the soul of propriety, that you just don't know how to tell a lie and that you'd be miserable if we didn't do things by the book. So, will you marry me, Melly?'

'I . . . this feels like a lifetime of Christmasses come at once,' she said breathlessly. 'Can it be true?'

He gazed down at her radiant face for a long time, then he closed his eyes and buried his head in her hair, and she clung to him rapturously.

'You still haven't said yes, Melly,' he murmured finally.

'Yes, Clay,' she whispered, 'I'd love to marry you . . .'

It was only when she was about to climb into bed after Clay had gone, to end what had become a shining day after all, that she suddenly remembered Tiffany's cat.

And she started in surprise and remembered it was still shut in the kitchen although it hadn't made a sound.

'My God,' she muttered. 'I hope it hasn't climbed out of the window and got stuck somewhere or fallen!'

But when she rushed to the kitchen and flung open the door, it was to find the cat curled up, fast asleep on the table.

'Well!' she said.

'So Melly,' Clayton Forrester said to her just after lunch the next day, with a lurking smile, 'Do you still want to marry me?'

'Did you think I'd change my mind?'

He grimaced. 'Until the deed is done, that's your prerogative.'

'Well, I haven't changed my mind,' she conceded and set her coffee cup down on the low table between the two settees. She looked around the luxurious room which was in fact part of an hotel suite with a roof garden, and was vastly elegant and expensively furnished but somehow impersonal. 'I always wondered where you lived. I didn't think it would be in an hotel.'

'It's simpler,' he said gravely.

'Oh, Clay,' her cheek dimpled, 'you need a wife!'

'I thought you might have guessed why I was marrying you,' he murmured and shot her a look of pure wickedness.

'Because you were tired of hotel life?' she hazarded.

'Yes . . .'

'Well that's a pity because I think it would suit me down to the ground!' she said airily. 'Just think, no worries about staff or meals. Oh yes, it would suit me!'

'And you're a minx, my dear,' he said but with his eyes laughing. 'Come here.'

She came and when he'd kissed her thoroughly and leisurely, she curled up in his lap with her head on his shoulder and one hand slipped beneath his jacket. 'How long have you lived here, Clay?'

'Do you really want to know?'

'Mmm.'

'Since I spent a couple of nights here once and realised that a beautiful, elegant old hotel which was almost a landmark, was in dire straits and headed for demolition to make way for another shopping centre.'

'So you offered to help them out of their difficulties?'

'In a way—I bought it,' he said apologetically.

She laughed softly. 'You remind me of my father! He once bought me a bike which wasn't a great success. I mean it fell to pieces rather quickly, so he went out and bought the factory. And you've made it a success?' she added rather quickly. 'How?'

He didn't answer for a minute, then he said, 'I turned it into a place that was renowned for it's old-fashioned service. People like to come here and feel they're pampered—and they don't mind paying for it. Melly, don't you want to talk about your father?'

She stirred. 'It's not that.'

'What is it then? You weren't planning to marry me without him knowing were you?'

She looked up at him. 'Yes. Yes, I was,' she said slowly.

'Why?' His eyes narrowed. 'Don't you think he'd approve of me?'

'Oh yes! You're not only an answer to my prayers,' she murmured with a faint smile, 'but you'd be an answer to his too! He's desperately afraid someone will rush me off my feet and marry me for my money! But he certainly couldn't accuse you of that, could he?'

'Not the money bit, no. But if we do it without him knowing, he might think I rushed you off your feet.'

'Clay,' she hesitated, 'if we were to wait two months, and that's how long he'll be away for because for once in his life, he's mixing business with pleasure—mind you, only on doctor's orders! But he's gone on a cruise and then he's visiting a friend in America and they're going on a shooting vacation—but to get back, I can't see myself changing my mind if I did wait that long so there's no point.'

'And what about the people keeping an eye on you in his absence?'

'Well,' she thought for a bit, 'I think I could arrange to check in with them rather than have them check up on me—only because I wouldn't want them to get in touch with him and bring him tearing home!'

'Are you very sure this is how you want to do it, Melly?' he said quietly.

'Yes, Clay,' she whispered. And a minute or so later she said, 'There's another reason why I'd rather do it this way. I suspect my father will put up a bit of a fight about whoever I wanted to marry on the grounds that I'm too young, and I very much suspect that in his eyes, even when I'm thirty I'll still be too young to know my own mind. But although he worries about me very genuinely, he's left me alone to fend for myself for a long time now, in a sense. I mean physically, he's made sure I've been taken great care of, but mentally—well it hasn't always been that way. He sent me away after my mother died, when I needed—maybe we both needed each other very much.'

'It ... if you bear a grudge against your father, Melly,' Clay said as if he was choosing his words carefully, 'this might not be ...'

'No, Clay,' she interrupted, 'I don't bear him a grudge. He's ... just the way he is. But he's had the ordering of my life for a long time. Long enough. It's my turn now. And this is the way I want to do it. Do you know what I wish, really wish?' she said softly, and moved her hand beneath his jacket.

'What?'

'That we could just be like any ordinary couple. That we could find ourselves somewhere ... not grand, just nice to live and have some fun decorating it and for a while, pretend you're not Clayton Forrester and I'm not Melissa Heatley. I think that would be a very good way to start off our married life, don't you?'

He tilted her chin up and his eyes were very tender. 'So be it, Melly. If you're very sure ...'

'Now you're asking me that. Aren't you ... sure now?' Her eyes widened suddenly. 'Clay?'

'. . . Yes I'm sure,' he said with just a suggestion of a hesitation. But he countered that immediately by holding her close to him, so close she could barely breathe and then kissing her until she was dizzy with delight and she was sure that she'd imagined anything strange about him at all.

They were married ten days later.

It was a civil ceremony and again, no-one who knew Clayton Forrester or Melissa Heatley, knew about this. Not even Tiffany Evans. Melissa had insisted that she wasn't going to tell her until after the deed was done and had remained adamant even when Clay had teasingly asked her if she was ashamed of him somehow.

She'd also left everything up to Clay regarding what happened after the wedding, although she did wangle two weeks of unpaid leave from work. In fact she'd worked right up until lunchtime of her wedding day—it was a Saturday. Then she'd changed into the simple white dress she'd bought and he'd been waiting for her outside the office and driven her straight to the registry office, handing her, on the way, an exquisite little bouquet of pale violets that matched her eyes. Then they'd gone to his hotel, straight up to the penthouse suite with its roof-garden for a champagne lunch.

And all through lunch and later when he'd spent some time kissing her, her heart had been near to bursting with a mixture of joy and disbelief and just a dash of nervousness.

But finally he'd put her away from him and looked at her expectant face with a faintly wicked smile in his eyes. 'When are you going to tell Tiffany about us?' he murmured.

'Sometime today, I should, otherwise she'll worry. What . . . you said you had a surprise for me?'

'Mmm. But for now, how would it be if I dropped you off at the flat to collect your things and break the good tidings,' his eyes had glinted devilishly, 'and picked you up in say . . . an hour?'

'All right . . .'

'You've *what*!' Tiffany stared at Melissa incredulously. She tottered to a chair and sank down. 'I don't believe it,' she said weakly.

'Look at this then.' Melissa showed her her wedding ring.

'Oh my God.' Tiffany sprang up. 'But what about your father? Does he know . . . *Melissa* . . .' Her jaw worked but no further sound came.

'Tiffany,' Melissa said straightly, 'there's no earthly reason why he could object to Clay, now is there? You said yourself he was incredibly wealthy and very respected in financial circles. And he's obviously socially acceptable otherwise your parents, who are terribly sweet but awful snobs, wouldn't entertain him. And all that means that he can only have wanted to marry because he loves me. Besides . . .'

'All right, all right! But by the same token, there's no reason to have done it secretly, is there?'

'Yes there was,' Melissa said with a look of unusual stubbornness in her lavender-blue eyes. 'For so long now you've all treated me like the original innocent, it's become a habit. And I could just picture that out of *sheer* habit, you would all assume I didn't know what I was doing and accordingly try to talk me out of it. But I know exactly what I'm doing and what's more, it's done! And . . . oh, Tiff,' she said with a sudden break in her voice, 'be happy for me please. I love him so much and I feel as if I've . . . come home . . .'

'Melissa!' Tiffany put her arms around her suddenly, 'Oh honey . . . yes I am happy for you, I am, love. It's just, well, it came as a bit of a shock.' She lifted her head and looked at the wall opposite over Melissa's shoulder and blinked and thought, you can say that again!

'Then you'll help me, Tiff?'

'Help you,' Tiffany said warily although she still hugged Melissa. 'You don't mean . . . break the news to your father?'

'No.' Melissa giggled and pulled away. 'I mean help me to keep it a secret a little bit longer.' She explained about her father being on the first real holiday he'd taken in years and how she didn't want the news to reach him circumspectly. 'I plan to check in with his secretary and Nanny Ellen and so forth but just in case they ring here or turn up here will you tell them I'm out or something like that? It will only be for a few more weeks.'

Tiffany studied Melissa's expectant face. 'Yes,' she said, 'God help me. On one condition, that you don't shut me out of this marriage as you did out of the courtship. I want to know where you're going to live and I expect to be a frequent guest!'

'You will,' Melissa said fervently, 'you will.'

Then Clay knocked on the door and Melissa let him in a little shyly.

'Tiffany,' he said, 'we've met I think.'

'Yes we have.' She looked at him, unable to disguise the curiosity in her eyes. Then the awkward moment was broken in an unexpected way. The Persian cat which had been slumbering on the settee, woke up, washed it's face sleepily then took a flying leap into Clayton Forrester's arms.

'Well!' Tiffany said.

CHAPTER FIVE

'THAT address you gave to Tiffany,' Melissa said to Clay when they'd left the flat and were driving along, 'is it where we're going to live?'

'That depends on you.'

'Clay, you're being awfully mysterious!'

'Well, you did say you would leave it up to me.'

'I know but . . .'

'Hold hard, sweetheart,' he interrupted. 'We're nearly there.'

And ten minutes later he pulled the car into the kerb in the suburb of Darlinghurst, in a street lined with trees and two rows of beautiful old terrace houses.

'Do you mean . . .'

She looked up at the two-storied house they were parked outside of, with its lacy wrought-iron verandah railings and cherry red front door.

'Is it ours?' she said uncertainly.

'Yes. Do you like it? I must warn you it's not quite finished. But all the structural repairs have been done and it's liveable. But it's only very basically furnished . . . ten days isn't a long time in which to work miracles. And I thought you'd want to finish it off yourself anyway.'

'Oh Clay,' she whispered. 'How did you know?'

'You told me, Melly.'

'And you don't mind us living just like an ordinary couple? I mean . . . your life must be . . .'

'Was overdue for a change,' he said with a lurking smile.

'I didn't expect you to ... I ...' She stopped and sniffed. 'It's just what I had in mind. Oh Clay.'

'Don't cry.'

'I ... it's only because I'm so happy!'

He pulled her close and kissed her forehead. 'Then you may cry,' he said softly. 'But I can't help wondering what you do when you're sad.'

'I suppose I cry too,' she said tremulously. 'No I don't. At least I cry much more easily when I'm happy. That's strange, isn't it? Are you going to carry me over the doorstep?'

But later, a lot later, she was thinking, only I could do this. Maybe they weren't so wrong about me after all.

'Melly, is something wrong?'

She stared upwards in the dark, afraid suddenly to even speak. It can't be happening to me, she thought desperately.

They were lying side by side in the bed which was one of the few pieces of furniture in the house and she was wearing a frothy confection of a nightgown, and it had been all right up until only a short time ago. They'd unpacked some of their things and then gone out to a corner store to buy some supplies and wandered into a pub on the way home and had a few drinks before coming back to the house to make an omelette for supper.

But all the time alongside her love and joy, something else had been insidiously growing within her—nerves, she'd told herself. They say it hurts the first time. Besides which, compared to the likes of ... Carmen Beresford, I'll probably seem awfully ... tame, to him. Oh God! Take a deep breath ...

Many deep breaths had not helped her, however, when it had looked as if he was going to undress her, and she'd made some silly excuse to do it herself. And now she was lying beside him with her insides knotted up, trying just to breathe evenly so that she could speak at least.

'No, I love you,' she said tremulously. 'Only . . .'

He pushed himself up on one elbow. 'Melly . . .'

She moved precipitously. 'Clay, I feel sick,' she whispered. 'I'm so *sorry* . . .'

She only just made it to the bathroom. And to add, if anything, to her humiliation, Clay was there beside her, holding her, and when it was over, rocking her in his arms until the sweat on her forehead dried. Then he sponged her face and hands gently, wetting her nightgown in the process though, but he unbuttoned it and slid it off her body deftly and impersonally, and he reached behind the bathroom door for her white terry-towelling, short robe, and put her into it as if she was a stunned child.

Then he picked her up and carried her back to the bed and laid her in it. He switched on the bedside lamp which was on the floor and pulled another pillow behind her and covered her up. 'I'll be right back,' he murmured. 'Don't go away.'

He came back with two glasses and the bottle of brandy he'd bought at the pub, together with the wine he'd bought to have with their supper.

She didn't move but her eyes, which were huge and dark, followed his every move.

'Brandy's very good for settling stomachs,' he said and sat down beside her. 'Sit up.'

She sat up obediently and sipped from the glass he held to her lips. And coughed a little as the fiery liquid slid down her throat. 'Some more,' he said, and she sipped again. 'All right, lie back.'

She did so like a mechanical doll and he picked up one of her hands and massaged it.

'Melly . . .'

'Clay . . .'

He smiled slightly. 'You go first.'

'. . . I feel such a fool,' she said starkly and two tears slid down her cheeks.

'You shouldn't. You told me once you only got sick on the very best, most exciting occasions—like the Yass Show.' The corner of his mouth quirked. 'If I've lived up to that, I feel complimented.'

She stared up at him and felt herself beginning to smile, although reluctantly. 'Do you mean that? You're not just trying to make me feel better?'

'Yes I am trying to make you feel better and yes, I meant it.' He grinned down at her and she caught her breath.

But then his eyes sobered and he said very quietly, 'You don't have to be frightened of me, Melly. The last thing on earth I want to do is hurt you. But if you're stiff and tense and frightened, then these things do hurt more than they should. And we'd be better to wait until you feel more relaxed.'

'I did . . .' She stopped and bit her lip. 'I did feel a bit nervous,' she said in a gruff little voice. 'But really because I feel like such a novice compared to . . . well, you must have done this a thou . . . lots of times before and with . . . oh damn!' she said, as he started to laugh softly.

'Melly, oh Melly,' he breathed then and lay down beside her to gather her into his arms. 'You're so special, you know. No,' he held her very close as a tremor wracked her body, 'don't feel like that. Because I have to tell you I'm a bit nervous too.'

She moved a little away to stare up at him incredulously.

'Yes I am. You see, despite having done this—I wouldn't say thousands of times before,' he murmured wryly and brushed her forehead with his lips, 'but I can't deny I've done it before. Yet I've never done it with a virgin. So I need your help, sweetheart, you see. I need you to tell me if I'm going too fast for you, or if I'm hurting you.' He lifted a hand and traced the outline of her lips. 'In fact, that's always the best way to do it. Should we try that? I promise you, any time you want me to stop, I will.'

'Oh Clay,' she whispered, 'that makes me feel so much better. Yes let's . . . I love you so much.'

And she buried her head in his shoulder and didn't see the frown that came to his eyes, of what looked very much like pain. But it was gone as she moved in his arms and he let her go briefly so that he could untie the sash of her robe and slide his arms beneath it and gather her slender, delicate body close again.

The next few weeks had a distinctly dream-like quality for Melissa. She thought, after their wedding night that had started so disastrously, that she'd learnt so much, come into the possession of a kingdom of delight in fact, which had left her dizzy and shuddering with pleasure and clinging to Clay, at one with him in a way that not even her wildest imaginings had guessed at . . .

But as those first weeks passed, she learnt that there was more, far more to this kingdom, that her body was capable of even more pleasure, as he slowly and gently layer by layer, released her from the things she couldn't help but feel shy and nervous about. And her faith and trust in him grew day by day. ·

'Why are you looking at me like that?' he asked her one cold, bleak afternoon—another reminder that winter was on the way. Not that it was wintry within the lounge of their little house for a log fire burned brightly in the grate, and the new curtains which had only arrived the day before were closed. It was about three o'clock in the afternoon but the room was dim except for the firelight. So far there were only two chairs in the room, the settee was due to arrive tomorrow but there was a jewel-bright, hand-made rug in front of the fire which Melissa had found in a craft shop, and a coffee table.

And Clay was sitting on the rug, leaning back against one of the chairs with her in his lap. On the low coffee table were the remains of a late lunch she'd prepared in a hurry because she hadn't expected him home.

'How am I looking at you?' she murmured.

'As if you're afraid I might eat you, too.'

'Are you planning to?'

His eyes glinted and his lips twitched. 'In a manner of speaking. I didn't come home for lunch, you know.'

'No?' she said a little breathlessly.

'No.' His hand came up and those long strong fingers began unhurriedly to undo the buttons of her cardigan. 'I came home because I kept thinking how much I'd like to be doing this.' The last button gave way and he dealt with the buttons of her blouse just as deftly. 'You're very well dressed today, sweetheart,' he teased when he finally got through to her bra and fingered the front opening clasp.

'It's cold,' she whispered and shivered but not because she was cold. Then her bra gave way too and he pushed everything aside so that her high, pointed little breasts were revealed to gleam like warm ivory in the firelight.

'And this,' he said, barely audibly and bent his head to tease her nipples with his tongue.

'Clay . . . Clay, don't,' she said huskily, after a while.

'Why not? Don't you like it.'

'I . . . yes,' she said helplessly. 'But . . .'

He lifted his head and sent her a glance that was pure grey and rather wry. 'What is it, my little Puritan? Do you think we should confine these activities solely to night-time and bed? Or don't you think we should indulge in them at all?'

'I don't know,' she said shakenly. 'Is it right to feel so . . . for you to make me feel so . . .'

'Wanton?' he supplied.

'Something like that,' she whispered after a moment.

'It's very right, Melly,' he said gravely but she thought he was laughing at her all the same. 'Nor is it one-sided,' he added. 'I've been thinking of this all morning. So it would seem, you have the same effect on me.'

She slid her fingers through his hair. 'Then it isn't terribly sinful and positively decadent to feel like this?' she said just as gravely but with a smile lurking in her eyes.

'In our situation, married to each other as we are, it's very proper. It happens in the very best marriages,' he teased.

'Does it?' she said wide-eyed, 'at three o'clock

FREE

4 BOOKS AND A SURPRISE GIFT

Here's a sweetheart of an offer that will put a smile on your lips…and 4 free Harlequin romances in your hands. Plus you'll get a secret gift, as well.

As a subscriber, you'll receive 6 new books to preview every month. Always before they're available in stores. Always for less than the retail price. Always with the right to return the shipment and owe nothing.

YES

Please send me 4 **free** Harlequin Presents novels and my **free** surprise gift. Then send me 6 new Harlequin Presents each month. Bill me for only $1.75 each (for a total of $10.50 per shipment — a savings of $1.20 off the retail price) with no extra charges for shipping and handling. I can return a shipment and cancel anytime. The 4 free books and surprise gift are mine to keep!

106 ClP BA5U

NAME⎽⎽⎽⎽⎽⎽⎽⎽⎽⎽⎽⎽⎽⎽⎽⎽⎽⎽⎽⎽⎽⎽⎽⎽⎽⎽⎽⎽⎽⎽⎽⎽⎽⎽⎽

ADDRESS⎽⎽⎽⎽⎽⎽⎽⎽⎽⎽⎽⎽⎽⎽⎽⎽⎽⎽⎽⎽⎽⎽APT.⎽⎽⎽⎽⎽⎽

CITY⎽⎽⎽⎽⎽⎽⎽⎽⎽⎽⎽⎽⎽⎽⎽⎽⎽⎽⎽⎽⎽⎽⎽⎽⎽⎽⎽⎽⎽⎽⎽⎽⎽⎽⎽

STATE⎽⎽⎽⎽⎽⎽⎽⎽⎽⎽⎽⎽⎽⎽⎽⎽ZIP CODE⎽⎽⎽⎽⎽⎽⎽⎽

Offer limited to one per household and not valid for present subscribers.
Prices subject to change.

AS A HARLEQUIN SUBSCRIBER, YOU'LL RECEIVE FREE...

- our monthly newsletter **Heart To Heart**
- our magazine **Romance Digest**
- special-edition **Harlequin Bestsellers** to preview for ten days without obligation

So kiss and tell us you'll give your heart to Harlequin.

RUSH

Harlequin Reader Service
2504 W. Southern Avenue
Tempe, Arizona 85282

Postage will be paid by addressee

BUSINESS REPLY CARD

First Class Permit No. 70 Tempe, AZ

DETACH AND MAIL THIS CARD TODAY.

on a working afternoon, on the floor?'

'Mmm. Why don't you take my tie off and undo *my* buttons and I'll show you . . .'

He started to show her and she forgot the floor and the time and her curious uncertainties and arched her slender, naked fire-gilded body to his with a fervour that was intensified until she wasn't at all sure whether it was pain or pleasure, as his hands roamed over her at will, stroking, cupping, exploring, lingering on her throat, her breasts, her tiny waist and the curve of her hips, the soft, silken, inner skin of her thighs.

'Clay . . .' She said his name over and over with just about every inflection in her voice she was capable of, and then he said her name, deep in his throat and took her just when she thought she might die if he didn't.

But afterwards, she was unwittingly shy with him again.

'Still worried, Melly?' he said later when they were back in front of the fire, drinking the tea he'd made while she'd showered.

She shrugged her slim shoulders clad in her white terry robe and turned faintly pink.

He came to sit beside her and she caught her breath because it still seemed hard to believe that this tall man with his clever face and sometimes cynical eyes, whose hands and mouth were so very sure when they touched her, could really be her husband.

'Melly,' he said, and made her look at him with his fingers beneath her chin. 'There is nothing wrong,' he said very quietly and with his eyes completely serious, 'in anything two people do to each other that gives them pleasure.'

'I . . . I know that,' she stammered.

'Do you really?' he murmured. 'I don't think you know as much about it as you think. Otherwise you wouldn't look just a little shocked at times, at the things I do to you.'

'That's because . . . I told you I was a hick,' she whispered. 'And you're right,' her cheek dimpled although there was a shimmer of tears in her eyes, 'I don't know much about it at all. I didn't know I was going to feel . . . so much. I just didn't know you would be able to make me . . . want you so much. Much more than I ever dreamt and I had some pretty wild dreams about you,' she confessed. 'And sometimes too,' she added, 'I wonder if I shouldn't be . . . well, cooler about it in case I might seem to you—sort of clumsy and . . . like a schoolgirl let loose in a candy store. And sometimes I think that you do so much for me, but I don't do very much for you. I mean you do all the work . . .'

'Oh God, Melly,' he broke in on a suddenly tortured breath and when her eyes widened, he smiled, a curiously twisted smile and he touched her mouth gently.

'Have I said something wrong?'

'No . . . no.' He closed his eyes briefly. 'If I do all the work at the moment it's because I want to and that's the way it should be. You'll learn, and in the meantime, it pleases more than you might know, to do it. As for you being . . . cooler about it, I'd hate that so don't even think about it again. And as for me making you want me, well,' his eyes were suddenly very bright and tender, 'I do that because I want *you* very much. So you see, you don't have anything to worry about. You're doing fine, sweetheart. So well in fact . . .' But he didn't finish because she was crying and laughing and she spilt her tea on the rug although she didn't realise it, and for that matter, he didn't either.

And as she gained confidence, the house began to take shape, colourfully in some rooms, restfully in others and the walled courtyard at the back came alive with potted plants and a birdbath. It was quite small, the house, with a lounge and dining room and kitchen downstairs and two bedrooms and a bathroom upstairs. She did the lounge in whites and creams to make it look larger with only the hand-made rug before the hearth as a bright statement of colour but the dining room was a different matter. The walls she papered in a red paper that had a tiny white design on it and the chair seats and backs were covered with a matching fabric. The chairs themselves she'd found in a second-hand furniture shop together with an oval table and they'd all revealed themselves as genuine silky oak beneath layers of dust and cobwebs. She'd also found an old man who repaired furniture.

'I knew they had to be something special,' she said to Clay as she caressed the intricately carved, newly polished backs of one of the chairs. 'Aren't they lovely?'

He agreed.

'Do you like the room?'

Clay looked round, at the white marble fireplace, carefully restored from beneath a disfiguring coat of paint, at the beaten silver vase on a narrow serving table which held a fluffy cloud of white chrysanthemums, and at the very old silver candlesticks on the oval table. 'Yes. It's you,' he said. 'It has class.'

'Thank you, oh wise one!' she replied demurely

but with an impish glint in her eyes, and put her hands together in front of her. 'Would this classy but very humble wife, this worthless creature really, be able to interest her lord and master in taking dinner with her in this very ordinary, worthless room she has created?'

'What's wrong with having it on the coffee table in the lounge?' he asked gravely. 'We've been doing that since we moved in.'

'Ah! Coffee table in lounge very often lead to sitting on rug in lounge which very often lead to . . . other things not good for digestion but of course good for . . . well, very, very good but not good for digestion!'

'This lord and master does not agree,' he said impassively. 'This lord and master in fact, suspects worthless but classy wife has subtle plans to feed him so well on this dining-room table that he will lose all ambitions connected with rug in lounge. Yet wasn't it Confucius who said eat, drink *and* be merry?'

'It was not!' she protested. 'Confucius said, lord and master can eat like a civilised human being at dining-room table and still be very sexy! That's what he said.'

'Then Confucius was wrong,' Clay said softly but with a wicked grin as he reached for her. 'Probably because he never met you. If he had, he would have known that it's almost impossible to concentrate on anything else when you're around which is why, eating in the lounge with the rug handy, is a very practical thing to do. Do you think I don't know why you bought that rug?'

She dissolved into helpless laughter. 'I did not!'

'Yes you did.' He kissed her hair and her throat.

'It was the very first thing you bought and it was a brilliant idea.'

'Then, are you trying to tell me I went to all the trouble to decorate the dining room for nothing?'

'No. We'll keep it for guests . . .'

Which they more or less did and Tiffany was their first guest.

'I love it, I love it!' she said enthusiastically of the house.

And a little later, 'Oh Melissa, that fortune invested in your education which I was rather scathing about, was worth every penny—this food is divine!'

Melissa's cheek dimpled. 'Thank you.'

'Did you do it all yourself? I might have known,' Tiffany said with a touch of irony. 'I hope you realise,' she added to Clay, 'that Melissa is a far more determined, independent person than we tend to give her credit for.'

'Because I can make Asparagus Crêpes and Baked Fish with Lobster Sauce and a Chocolate Torte?' Melissa murmured whimsically before Clay could answer.

'In a sense,' Tiffany said ruefully. 'But you know what I mean.' She looked at them both in turn.

Clay lay back in his chair, his lids half-lowered over the grey of his eyes as he twirled his wine glass and watched the golden liquid settle. 'Yes I know what you mean, Tiffany,' he said at last and looked at her fully. 'That it would be a mistake to underestimate Melissa.'

For a brief moment Tiffany looked uncomfortable and Melissa wondered why and discovered that there was an undercurrent of something she didn't understand flowing between Clay and her best friend.

But Clay himself broke the unfathomable tension of the moment. He smiled at Tiffany and raised his glass slightly. 'It's an honour to have you here as our first guest. In our different ways we have the same interest at heart I think,' he murmured.

And Tiffany smiled slowly and raised her glass. 'Now, Melissa,' she said immediately as Melissa looked faintly bewildered, 'take me upstairs so we can have a little chat about things Clay wouldn't be at all interested in! We'll be back!' she promised Clay and pushed her chair away from the table.

'Is something wrong?' Melissa said anxiously when she and Tiffany were upstairs.

'No. Not so far as I know. There have been no private detectives sniffing around trying to find out where Melissa Heatley—that was, is,' she said humourously. 'And I can see,' she added softly, 'that Melissa Forrester is very, very happy. Which helps my conscience, I must say. I mean if I ever have to face your father, God forbid, I can say to him, look at her! Have you ever seen her so lovely or radiant! In other words, all's well that ends well.'

'You're a wonderful friend, Tiff,' Melissa said emotionally, and hugged her.

'Are you back at work?' Tiffany asked a few minutes later. She was seated at Melissa's dressing table repairing her make-up.

'Yes. I have been for a few weeks.'

'Do they know?'

'Not yet.' Melissa twisted her wedding ring which she took off and hung on a chain round her neck when she went to work, and when she went to see her father's secretary.

'And Clay?'

'I don't think he ever stops working completely,' Melissa said with a grin, 'although during the first two weeks he took a lot of time off—most of the time off. And he hasn't made any trips since we were married. But honestly, Tiff, that's a side of him I hardly know anything about and I don't really want to know about. I suppose that sounds strange to you but I . . .' she hesitated, 'I just wanted us to be like any ordinary couple for as long as we can. It—I don't know, but it seems really important to me. And so far it's worked out wonderfully well!' Her eyes shone.

Tiffany made as if to speak but in the end she didn't, just hugged Melissa again.

And it was only later that night when she was home again and sitting with the Persian cat in her lap, that Tiffany Evans voiced her reservations—to her cat.

'It can't go on like that for ever, of course, cat,' she mused. 'But then I'm obviously a poor judge. I never for one minute believed he'd marry her. Yet, incredibly, he must have fallen in love with her. Then again, why should that be so incredible? She's gorgeous and . . . but very young. Too young for him one would have thought. He could have had the best . . . frequently did in fact. Look at Carmen Beresford and Monique Carlisle—they say she took an overdose and had to have her stomach pumped out when he ended their relationship. And look at Tanya Miller, they've been friends for years. So many of them, cat. All beautiful, experienced worldly women who've made their mark what's more, intellectually. Yet he's married Melissa Heatley and appears to be quite content to be living in a little two-up, two-down house just like any ordinary married couple. Love is a strange thing, cat. Mind you, I should be applauding. Because it means there's hope for us, naive little girls . . . Perhaps I should really take a leaf out of Melissa's book. Borrow that look of lovely, shining innocence. After all I'm only ten months older.' She sighed suddenly. 'What do you say, cat?' she demanded.

Two months after Melissa and Clay were married, Melissa discovered her father was due to arrive home that day and about three weeks earlier than he was due.

She arranged to take the afternoon off from work and rang Clay to tell him she was going to see him.

'Melly,' his voice came rather sharply down the line, 'don't.'

'Why not?'

'Because I'd rather I spoke to him first.'

'Oh Clay,' her cheek dimpled, 'that's nice of you but he's not going to disinherit me or anything like that. He'll be cross for a little while but I know how to handle him. And I think it's something I should do.'

'Then wait—I can't get away at the moment but we can do it together tonight.'

'No we can't, he's driving down to Glen Morris tonight. He won't eat me, Clay. Don't worry about me. See you soon,' she said softly. 'I'll go straight home afterwards.' And she put down the phone gently and didn't hear the savage sound of exasperation he made.

She met her father's plane and was happy to see

him looking fit and tanned and rested. And she broke the news of her marriage to him in the back seat of the vast, black limousine which was at the airport to pick him up. She did it there because she couldn't wait any longer to tell him and there was a glass partition between the chauffeur and the back seat, for privacy.

But an hour later she got out of the car, which had been driving around aimlessly for some time at her father's direction, with her face white and stunned.

And the last words she said to her father were, 'It's not true! He loves me . . . he does.' Then she was running, running to get away from all that had been said in the back seat of that car, a shocking litany she couldn't believe . . .

But as she ran and then slowed to a stumbling walk, she knew with a terrifying bleakness that at least part of it was true, it had to be because it explained so many things.

And finally she stopped walking and looked around dazedly and then at her watch. It was only three o'clock. Clay would still be tied up so at least she could go home and think. She hailed a taxi.

But she couldn't think when she got home. She could only sit huddled in the cold lounge with one thought beating at her brain. He never . . . actually *said* he loved me. He never said the words. But it can't be true that he married me because . . . because . . .

A sound behind her made her lift her tear-streaked face suddenly, and look around.

It was Clay. An unfamiliar looking Clay with his face pale too, and his thick dark hair ruffled as if he'd been walking. But it was his eyes that made her heart go stone cold with fear. They were bleak, like the colour of frozen water. And she thought, is it true? Is it . . . oh God help me, don't do this to me, don't . . .

Then she was talking, unbelievably she was saying, 'I didn't expect you home so soon. I . . .'

'Melly,' he said harshly. 'Let's not play games. You know, don't you?'

'I . . . know some things,' she whispered. 'I couldn't believe them at first. But they have to be true.'

'Tell me.'

'I . . .'

'Tell me what your father said.' His voice was flat but commanding. He walked over to the fireplace and struck a match so that the paper beneath the logs caught alight and within moments a streak of flame shot up. Then he opened the antique corner cupboard that had been her pride and joy because it was made of rosewood and had the most beautiful lattice front and she'd picked it up for a song and her old friend who repaired furniture had brought it back to its glowing, original beauty; and he took a glass and a bottle out of it and poured her a neat brandy.

'I'm not feeling sick.'

'Drink it, Melly.'

She sipped the brandy. 'Melly,' she said slowly. 'Melissa, Melisande—he told me a story, the kind of story you wouldn't read about. About a girl called Melisande who he loved . . . as he's never loved anyone since. But two weeks before they were due to get married, she ran away—this Melisande. She turned her back on James Heatley despite all his wealth and noble,' she lifted her eyes briefly, 'your word I think, Clay, lineage, and ran away with one of his employees of all things and *they* got married. But try as he would, James Heatley couldn't forget her. Not even years later when he married Barbara McGovern, although he tried. He said he tried.' Melissa took a gulp of her brandy. 'She was my mother, Barbara McGovern. And she was in love with my father, that's why he married her—so he said. She was also of true yeoman stock, so he said too, and utterly dependable. Which was just as well, wasn't it, Clay? That she had her yeoman stock to fall back on otherwise she might have gone out and shot herself when she realised what she'd got herself into. But she didn't know at first. She didn't really know until I was about two years old, apparently, and some thoughtless friend said to her—I'm surprised you agreed to the name of Melisande for your baby.'

'Go on,' Clay said after a while.

Melissa drank some more brandy. 'All right. But she'd already begun to think, to wonder why her marriage wasn't working out that well ... he told me this. He *knew* what she was thinking. Then this friend said what she did, spilt the beans, and my mother confronted my father and asked him if he'd really christened *their* daughter after a girl he'd loved and couldn't forget. He didn't deny it. He told her everything, how this Melisande had made it impossible for him to really love anyone else. My mother took stock—at least that's what I presume she did. He didn't say if she ranted or raved ... or felt cold, so cold. All he said was that they came to a decision. For my sake, they would continue this ... loveless marriage.'

She stood up. 'At least what then became a marriage in name only. She made that stipulation, probably because she was so hurt, I don't know.

I'll never know. But that's what they did. Oh, and she made one other stipulation. That I was never to be called Melisande again—after *your* mother.'

There was silence, broken only by the hissing of the fire. Until Clay said, 'Did he tell you what he did to *my* father?'

'Yes,' she said tonelessly. 'He had him sacked . . .'

'He did more than that, Melly. He made damned sure he never got another job that was anything approaching the kind of job he was fitted for. He smeared his reputation beyond repair—my father was a research chemist which is a fairly closed kind of world, so it wasn't hard for someone as powerful as James Heatley to do that. And my father lived the rest of his life in a torment of frustration and my mother—well, she fretted her life away in an anguish of guilt that I never understood until she died and then my father told me the whole story. And on that day, I made a vow that I would avenge them both.'

Melissa flinched visibly and stared blindly at the fire through a mist of tears. 'So he was right about the rest of it, too,' she whispered.

Clay took so long to answer, she thought he wasn't going to, and something within her withered and died.

Then he said, 'That's debatable.'

'No, Clay,' she wept, 'I think that's got to be as true as the rest of it. He said the only reason you would have married me was for revenge, to get back at *him*. He said that,' she swallowed, 'that men like you don't marry little girls like me. He even quoted me a list of names, of women you've lived with and told me what they were like, how different they were . . . to me. And when I tried to tell him how we've been, he laughed and said, of course! That I'd be a g-gorgeous novelty t-to,' her voice shook, 'to take to bed and there wouldn't be many men who would think otherwise. But that you'd get tired of me pretty soon, and that's when I'd start to pay on *his* behalf. And that's how you'd get your revenge.'

'Melly . . .' Clay's voice was strange, a mixture of harshness and compassion and he hesitated briefly, and she felt as if there was a knife in her breast turning slowly and knew that she would give it the final twist.

'Clay, tell me this,' she said huskily. 'When you found out who I was, did you . . . decide to make me fall in love with you?'

He was looking at the fire as she spoke. Then he turned his head and his grey gaze flickered over her. 'Yes,' he said quietly. 'I did. If he hadn't . . . if he hadn't had the audacity to call you after her, after *wrecking* her life, and my father's, I might not have. But that really got to me. That . . . seemed to open it all up again. And I thought suddenly, well, well! Little does he know it, but an unexpected tool has presented itself to me in the shape of his very own daughter, whom he actually called Melisande. Poetic justice that, I thought. So yes, Melly,' his eyes held hers captive, 'I can't deny that I set out to make you fall in love with me. Because I knew he would hate that.'

She stood like a stone statue. Then she whirled on her heel and tried to run from the room but he was too quick for her. He caught her at the doorway and when she tried to wrench herself free, he said through his teeth, 'Don't. You'll only get hurt.'

'Hurt!' she wept. 'There's nothing left of me to hurt, Clay.'

He picked her up and carried her over to the settee and sat her down, and sat down beside her, imprisoning her. 'Look, let's get some things straight,' he said brusquely. 'In theory, it's quite some time since I stopped congratulating myself for what I was doing to you. But I've lived with this thing for a long time. In fact at one stage, it was the whole motivating force in my life. Some people credit me with a touch of genius but if anything it was that from the day I left school, I worked my guts out to better myself and to achieve wealth and with it, the same kind of power your father wielded because I knew that was the only way I could . . . meet him on equal ground, at least. Can you understand that?'

Even in her misery Melissa had to acknowledge to herself that she understood some things at least. She'd been right about the unhappy childhood for one thing, and the sort of darkness in his soul she'd seen fleetingly sometimes but been unable to pin down. Not that it helped her . . .

'Yes,' she said in a despairing whisper. 'But . . .'

'But once I got to know you, even while I was no longer applauding myself,' he said grimly, 'there was a . . . compulsion about it that wouldn't let me stop although I tried to, once notably, at least. When I found out you were prepared to marry me without telling your father—that made me stop and think. I hadn't expected that, I hadn't expected it to be nearly as easy as that. And I thought then,' he looked away briefly, 'well, let's say I did battle with my conscience then. But the compulsion won. And part of that compulsion sprang from you yourself, Melly,' he said intently.

'You may be only a child by comparison to others I've known, but you're an enchanting, bewitching child and it hasn't exactly been a penance to be married to you—as I think you must have known.'

She stared up at him, her eyes huge and dark and wet, like violet puddles in her white face. 'If that's supposed to make me feel better,' she said desolately, 'it doesn't. Nor does it solve anything. You don't love me, it's as simple as that.'

'I doubt if love is ever that simple,' he said dryly. 'And I've come to . . . care very much about you and what happens to you.'

'Because I'm such a gullible child?' she said bitterly. 'Then my father's right. That won't take the place of love for long.'

'And I've no doubt he'll be wildly disappointed if I don't turn out quite as black as he's painted me,' Clay said in a hard voice.

She made a small sound in her throat but he went on relentlessly, 'Anyway, I wonder if we should quote him on the subject?'

'What do you mean?' she whispered.

'I mean, I wonder if he really knows what love is?'

'Do you? Know what it is, Clay?'

He stood up and his eyes were colder than she'd ever seen them. 'No. I'm not sure what it is, Melly,' he said very quietly. 'Sometimes I wonder if it even exists or if it isn't just a term that's come to be used for a whole lot of baser emotions. For instance, was it love that your father felt for my mother? Was it love that precipitated everything that's happened since? If you'll forgive me for saying so,' he looked at her ironically, 'I could think of another name for it, like hurt pride.'

Melissa trembled. What can I say? she thought

dully. I feel . . . just destroyed; just so hopeless and helpless to think that he only cares for me because he thinks of me as a vulnerable child—but that's the way people feel for stray dogs and orphans. How can I live with that?

She took a deep, unsteady breath. 'All right,' she said in a queer little voice. 'Where do we go from here? You must have realised how I'd feel when I found all this out. Did you have a "plan of action" for that too?'

'No, I didn't have a plan of action,' he said with a ruthless kind of mockery that made her bite her lip and realise how feeble her own attempt at mockery had sounded.

He went on. 'In fact, I didn't believe your father would tell you the whole story—a miscalculation on my part, I admit.' His lips twisted. 'Oh,' he added as her eyes widened, 'I knew he'd cut up rough, but I didn't think he'd humble himself sufficiently to tell you, truthfully, why. So no, I didn't make a plan. As a matter of interest, what do *you* think we should do?'

She licked her lips. 'Clay, there's no way we could go on. You're not thinking that, surely?' Her voice cracked.

'It's exactly what I'm thinking . . .'

CHAPTER SIX

'AND I let him talk me into it. Incredibly, I did . . .'

The apartment block where Tanya Miller lived was very quiet and so were the streets outside—so quiet that Melissa could hear some faint birdsong coming from a park two blocks away.

She pushed aside the bedclothes and wandered over to the window. But it was still pitch dark outside.

She rested her forehead on the cool glass, and thought back again.

'Yes, I let him talk me into it,' she murmured. 'I must have been mad. No, I think in my heart of hearts, I still hoped there might be a chance that he'd fall in love with me. And I wished, and hoped, and prayed that I was pregnant because I was stupid enough to think that would do it. But what was there to fall in love with?'

Not much, she mused. A nervous, colourless *child*. That's what I became. I lost all confidence, all conversation, I couldn't relax when he tried to make love to me—I couldn't relax at all. I couldn't stop thinking of what my mother must have gone through or what his mother must have gone through. But mostly, I couldn't accept that he still wanted to be with me for myself. I was obsessed with the thought that he didn't *love* me, and I couldn't accept that in fact he never changed towards me. That he was still the same Clay who could make me shiver and tremble with a look, could make any day of my life a better day just to see him. I couldn't accept that. I thought that with all I knew, he shouldn't be able to do that. But the awful truth was that he could. And I hated him, but mostly I hated myself because he could. And I was stiff and rebellious every time he made love to me after that so that it was more like war. Oh God . . .

'But how would you have felt?' she burst out suddenly and immediately looked around uneasily. Nothing appeared to disturb the quiet pre-dawn, though.

Yes, for instance you, Tanya, she mused. Wouldn't you have felt the same? Wasn't it just an impossible situation? It was for me. And then two things happened to make it more impossible —two things on the same day. About a month after my father came back I went shopping during my lunch hour, and quite by chance I happened to walk past the entrance to Clay's hotel. And on the front steps, who should I see but Clay himself, with a woman in his arms. And he was kissing her. It wasn't you, Tanya —oh! That's where I've heard your name before —you were one of the ones on my father's list! But never mind, it wasn't you. Maybe it was Carmen Beresford or Monique Carlisle, strange that I should have remembered their names after so long, they were on his list too. Or maybe it was someone new. She was very elegant. And he was holding her in his arms . . . well, I crept away, you see, because, for one thing, I *knew* how hopeless I'd been lately—I knew he was getting impatient with me not only in bed but out of it. I was so wrapped up in misery it must have been like living with a zombie. And I could tell from the odd things he said, things that cut me to the quick, that he was getting tired of it . . .

But he must have seen me scuttling away because he said to me over dinner that night . . .

'Melly, what you saw today . . .'

'You don't have to explain, Clay,' I interrupted. 'It's all going according to plan, isn't it?'

'Melly,' he said evenly, 'that was a good friend I hadn't seen for years, that's *all*.'

'If you say so,' I murmured.

His eyes smouldered suddenly. 'All right,' he drawled, 'believe what you want to believe. How's your father?'

'I don't know. I haven't seen him since . . . why do you ask?'

'I just wondered what kind of revenge *he* was planning, I'm sure he'll think of something.'

Melissa's mouth went dry. 'What do you mean?'

'Sweetheart,' he said deliberately, 'I thought of quite a few ways to harm his empire before you fell into my lap. And while he may be a lot of things, he's not a fool. So I should imagine he's thought up a few ways to bring me down by now. It should be quite a war,' he added idly . . .

'And that's when I knew I had to go,' Melissa said out aloud and jumped at a sound at the door. 'Tanya,' she said weakly after a moment. 'I'm sorry, did I wake you?'

'No.' Tanya walked into the room. 'I don't think you did. I just couldn't sleep so I decided to come and see if you were all right. Which you're not.'

'I am, really,' Melissa protested but her gaze fell before Tanya's acutely probing eyes. 'It's only that seeing Clay again, has made me . . . go over it all again, you see.'

'Yes,' Tanya said slowly. 'I see. Listen why don't you get back into bed and I'll make us something to drink. I'll be back in a tick.'

She was, with two cups of steaming cocoa. 'Are you comfortable?' she asked as she set them down on the bedside table and leant behind Melissa to adjust the pillows. Then she pulled up a chair beside the bed. 'Go on,' she said softly.

Melissa blinked. 'What . . .?'

'You said you were going over it all again. Had you finished?'

'No, not quite but . . .'

'Honey, sometimes there's nothing so good for you as to *tell* someone. Have you ever done that?'

'No but . . .'

'You don't think I'm the right person to tell?' Tanya looked wry.

'It's not that,' Melissa said going faintly pink.

'I think it is,' Tanya replied quietly. 'Maybe I should tell *you* a bit about me and Clay.'

Melissa looked away, but Tanya went on steadfastly, 'I've known him for a long time, for years and years because we were at night-school together. I was studying art when he was just finishing his accountancy course. We were good friends but nothing more—then. That didn't come until later after I'd . . . virtually ruined my life. Oh, I won't bore you with the details, but if it hadn't been for Clay I'd never have made it back. He . . . literally picked up the pieces, and we lived together for awhile and somehow or other, he managed to give me back my self-respect, not only for myself but for my painting too.'

She stopped and Melissa found herself unwittingly waiting for her to go on. 'Then we parted,' Tanya said finally. 'I think we both thought of getting married and I think we both discarded the idea because . . . well, we did. But the lovely part of it was that we parted with no regrets—just enormous mutual respect and a lot of liking. I went overseas and I've never looked back since, all thanks to Clay. And, we've seen each other again, over the years, and every time we do, someone manages to link our names romantically,' she said humourlessly. 'But it hasn't been—quite—so.'

Melissa clenched her hands together.

'I know,' Tanya said evenly. 'What you saw yesterday seems to make a liar of me but can I tell you what really happened? Until a few days ago I hadn't seen Clay for . . . over three years, and we met quite by accident. He was here on business. And I was shocked . . . at first he seemed like the same old Clay, but then I realised he wasn't. He was harder and in an undefinable way, he looked older—he, beneath the surface, he'd really changed. So, because I'll always care what becomes of him, I set out to find out why he'd changed.'

Even the birds have gone back to sleep, Melissa thought, as not a sound was to be heard. 'Did he tell you?' she asked at last.

'Not willingly,' Tanya said. 'In fact he laughed at me and said my imagination was working overtime. In *fact* it was by accident that I found out. He took me out to dinner and in the course of conversation I said jokingly, something about that he was leaving it rather late to get married and didn't he think it was time to put half the female population of Australia out of their misery? He said, flatly, I am married. Which as you can imagine shook me rigid, Melissa.'

Melissa didn't say anything.

Tanya went on. 'And I suppose, having said that, he thought he might as well tell me the rest. It didn't make pretty hearing.'

'Did he tell you about my father . . . what did he tell you?'

'That for some reason which he didn't go into, he'd felt he'd had pretty good cause to hate your father and want to hurt him. And he told me how he'd done it. He also told me how you'd reacted and how you'd disappeared.'

They stared at each other. Then Melissa said shakily, 'I think I had pretty good cause to.'

'Yes,' Tanya agreed. 'And you've also had . . . your revenge. I'm not saying that Clay didn't deserve to pay, but I think he's been paying every day since you left.'

'Because he's had me on his conscience,' Melissa whispered. 'He needn't have . . .'

'That's undoubtedly a reason,' Tanya interrupted. 'Only someone with no feelings whatever, would not have worried. Look, I'm not trying to excuse what he did. But I am trying to say that's not the whole Clay. And I think what motivated him in the first place, must have been very deep-rooted, very much felt . . .'

'Yes it was,' Melissa said.

'Then don't you think you could find it in your heart to forgive him now?'

'I . . . I forgave him a long time ago . . .'

'Is that why you're going through this kind of hell now?' Tanya said wisely.

'I wouldn't be if I hadn't had the misfortune to knock on your door yesterday.'

'Because of . . .'

'No,' Melissa said quietly, 'not because of you, if that's what you were going to say.'

Tanya looked at her piercingly. Then she murmured, 'I'm glad to hear you say that. Because you see, the fact that Clay spent the night with me, has no place in this at all. It came about as my way of offering him some warmth and comfort— which he seemed to need. That's all it was.'

Melissa shivered involuntarily.

'You haven't had much warmth and comfort for a long time, have you, Melissa?'

The words hung in the air between them.

'I haven't needed it,' Melissa said honestly. 'I ... since I lost his ...' She stopped abruptly.

Tanya's green eyes narrowed. 'Not ... lost his baby? Oh, my dear ...'

'I ... shouldn't have said that. You mustn't ... tell him. Promise me.'

'Tell me about it.'

'I ... couldn't believe it at first. I didn't know I was pregnant when I left. And then for a while, I thought I was late because I'd been in such a turmoil mentally. But finally I knew it was true and I couldn't help being, well, happy. Then when I was about four months pregnant, I fell down some steps. Actually, I got a fright. I was hurrying home after work—it was my fourth job in four months because I kept moving those first few months, and I thought these two men were following me—I thought they must either be working for Clay or my father. So I started to run and I tripped and fell all the way down this flight of stairs. The silly thing was though, they hadn't been following me at all because they came to my rescue and got me to hospital. But I lost the baby and the doctors said there might be some damage that would make it ... well, that I might never be able to have another one. After that,' she raised her eyes to Tanya's, 'it was easier. I just didn't feel much anymore. Which was a good thing because I was able to make a sort of a life. In fact,' she grinned faintly, 'in the last two years I've had quite an amazing life. I've done things I never thought I'd do, I've seen a lot of places ... and I've proved, I think,' she said very quietly, 'that no one needs to have me on their conscience. It may not be the kind of life Melissa Heatley was brought up to expect, or the kind of life James Heatley would want for his only daughter, but ... well, *you* said something about self-respect, so you might know what I mean. I don't depend on anyone, I don't need to. And that means a great deal to me.'

'I see,' Tanya said pensively, quite a while later.

'Do you think you do?' Melissa asked anxiously.

The other girl looked at her abstractedly. 'Yes. Yes, Melissa,' she added more positively. 'All right. For now though, I think you have to do as Clay wants you to do. Go with him to see your father.'

'I don't have to go with him ...'

'But don't you see,' Tanya murmured, 'if you expect Clay to believe you're a whole, independent person now, it's no use shying away from him all the time. If you do, he's going to think you're still deeply hurt, or that you're still in love with him. And knowing Clay,' she remarked, 'I don't think you'd get away from him this time.'

Melissa opened her mouth and shut it again.

'Exactly.' Tanya's green eyes glinted.

Melissa sighed heavily. 'All right,' she said. 'Where is he?'

'He's at an hotel. He rang me yesterday afternoon and last night, to find out how you were.'

'You've been very kind, Tanya. Making me stay the night and so on. I ... really didn't feel like being alone yesterday.'

'I know.' Tanya patted her hand. 'Tell you

what, do you think you could sleep now? Because you look as if you could do with it?'

'But what about . . .'

'Just give me the details, where you live and what you want organised etc., and Clay and I will take care of it.'

'Tired?' Clay said to her, much later that same day.

Melissa came out of her brown study with a start. They were driving along a narrow road that the moonlight had turned to a ribbon of silver as it wound between great paddocks of grass that were tinged with gold by the same full moon.

It was a road that she knew like the back of her hand and with every mile it was taking her closer to Glen Morris.

'A bit,' she said, and turned her head briefly to Clay.

They'd flown from Melbourne to Albury that afternoon and hired a car for the drive to Glen Morris. But there was something about the way he handled the car, something about the sight of his long powerful hands on the wheel, that disturbed her queerly and she turned away to look out over the moon-drenched landscape again.

Truth to tell, she felt deathly tired but in a way that had nothing to do with over-exertion, physically. But all to do with the stunning events of the past two days. It seemed almost beyond comprehension that she should be sitting in a car with Clay, driving to Glen Morris to see her father. But it was the implications of it that were just as stunning and the thought that kept hammering at her brain, was that she had to make her position perfectly clear, and keep doing it . . .

'Clay,' she said suddenly, and went on to his look of enquiry, 'I'm going to tell my father that there's no way you and I can simply take up where we left off. I think it's best to tell him straight away, don't you?'

He didn't answer for a long time. Then he said evenly, 'That's up to you, Melly.'

She thought for a bit. 'I should have thought it was the only thing to do—from both our points of view. Nothing's changed between us, has it?'

'If it has, we'll never know now, will we?' he said emotionlessly.

'But nothing *can* change your reason for marrying me, can it? The fact that you and my father have forgiven each other doesn't alter . . . us.'

He didn't reply and she didn't expect him to. So they drove the last few miles in silence.

Glen Morris was ablaze with light as they drove into the gravel forecourt. A dog barked imperatively but as Melissa got out of the car slowly, the streak of blue-grey that was hurtling towards her, pulled up short, skidding on the gravel. Then it came forward tentatively, its nose twitching and she said huskily, 'Red? It's me . . .'

Red, so called because he was a blue cattle dog but only red-headed people and red dogs are ever called Bluey, was delirious with delight. 'You didn't forget,' Melissa said with tears clogging her throat.

But then the dog was pushed aside and Melissa was enfolded in a pair of old, strong arms. 'Lass, oh lass,' Nanny Ellen groaned, 'd'yer ken what it means to see my baby again? How could you have done it?'

And Melissa found herself weeping into Ellen's shoulder 'I'm sorry . . . so sorry,' she wept.

'So long as you don't ever do it again!' Ellen Mackenzie said, her craggy face stern and forbidding. But then she, too, was crying and touching Melissa as if she couldn't believe she was real, and drawing her up the verandah stairs into the house, and making, quite unbeknown to Melissa, a resolve to start feeding her up because she'd gone thin—her baby!

But finally some equilibrium was restored and Melissa washed her face with cold water and brushed her hair and took a deep, deep breath. And allowed herself to be ushered into the upstairs bedroom where her father lay.

'He wanted to get up as soon as Mr Forrester rang but I wouldn't let him,' Ellen said aggressively. 'Anyone could see he wasn't well enough.' Her face softened though. 'But seeing you might do the world of good for him,' she added.

Melissa came downstairs a lot later and walked into the drawing room like someone walking in her sleep.

The room was very dim with only the moonlight shining on the polished surfaces of the beautiful old furniture to illuminate it.

She walked over to the bay window and just stood there with her hands hanging loosely at her sides, every line of her body betraying someone who was in the grip of a stunning sense of shock, someone who had not the faintest idea how to even begin to come to grips with it.

She didn't turn at the slight sound behind her. She didn't hear it and she had not the slightest idea that Clay was already in the room, standing with a cut-glass tumbler in his hand leaning his broad shoulders against the mantlepiece. Or that he'd watched her walk in, in silence.

Then a lamp sprang on and she turned convulsively and her eyes widened at the sight of his tall figure with his fingers still on the base of the lamp.

'Oh! It's you,' she said nervously and her hands suddenly clenched themselves into fists.

He said abruptly, 'You had better sit down. You look as if you've seen a ghost.'

She did and he crossed to the cocktail cabinet and poured her a stiff looking scotch. 'Your father is . . . it's come as a shock for you to see him like this. I'm sorry,' he said and handed her the glass but almost immediately took it from her as her hand shook, and put it down on a small table beside her chair. Then he sat down opposite her and looked at her, taking in her almost bloodless lips, his eyes narrowed and sombre.

'Yes . . .' she said with difficulty.

'Melly,' he said quietly, 'you mustn't give up hope. I've been in touch with his doctors today and they say they haven't yet. There is an operation apparently that's been pioneered in America which has a . . . reasonable success rate. And now there's someone in Australia who's studied the technique and the surgical procedures.' He hesitated. 'I don't want to get your hopes up unfairly but it's a chance.'

'I know. He told me,' she whispered. 'He also told me why he wouldn't go to America when he first learnt of it . . . why he's wasted so much time.'

'You mustn't blame yourself for that . . .'

'How can I *not*?' She closed her eyes and when

she opened them, the torture in them was plainly visible.

He stared at her with a frown of pain in his own eyes before he said finally and almost harshly, 'If you want to blame someone at least blame the right person, blame me.'

'No.' She took a quivering breath. 'No,' she said again and tried to take a sip of her whisky but her teeth chattered against the side of the glass and she put it down. 'He ... I ... you see, I thought I hated him because of what he'd done to my mother, to your mother—your father and you, and I still hate that but ...'

'But what?' he said finally when it seemed she couldn't go on.

She dropped her head into her hands.

'*Tell* me, Melly,' he said and there was something tight and coiled in his voice that might have frightened her if she hadn't been past that emotion.

She licked her lips and raised her head. 'For *all* that, he's my father,' she said at last. 'For sixteen years he was the light of my life just as much as my mother was. I don't know how to explain it but, well ...' She moistened her lips and a pulse beat steadily at the base of her throat. 'When he just took it for granted that we were reconciled, I didn't have the heart to disillusion him. He was so happy for me and he said that the thought of us reunited was giving him strength because he knew how much ... how much I loved you. And I just couldn't find the words to tell him the truth!' Her voice shook. 'Because I was so afraid he would start to feel guilty again and lose the will to fight this thing. You see, since I left—possibly since my mother died or maybe even before that, he's been battling so many guilts. He told me he'd been carrying a load of guilt and self-recrimination for years. And this is the only one he can ... assuage. And that's why I couldn't tell him.'

'I see ...'

'But do you understand what I've done, Clay?' she asked unhappily and with her eyes still mirroring her inner bewilderment.

He looked at her for a long time, seeing her confusion and bewilderment, and an echo of that air of incredulous shock with which she'd walked into the room ...

Then his lips twisted grimly. 'Yes, Melly, I see,' he said dryly. 'You've done the unthinkable—you've committed yourself to coming back to me.'

Their eyes locked. He was sprawled back in his chair and wearing the same charcoal grey suit he'd had on all day and he looked tired too, she thought suddenly.

'I ... there just doesn't seem to be anything else to do,' she said helplessly. 'Of course it won't be for real. I mean it can't, can it?'

He raised his eyebrows. 'Personally, I don't see how it can be any other way.'

She stared at him with her forehead knitted in a frown of intense concentration.

He shrugged at length. 'It's only a matter of being realistic I would have thought. We don't really know how long he'll be in this vulnerable condition, do we? I'm told this operation might only effect a partial recovery. He could be a semi-invalid for years. Are you planning for us to put on a loving act for years?'

Her lips parted but it was a while before she spoke. 'If necessary,' she said finally. 'People do it ... they do it for their children,' her eyes were suddenly bitter, 'so why can't we do it for a sick, maybe dying man? Oh, you can go your own way so long as he doesn't find out about it . . .' She stopped as he sat up abruptly.

'Thank you,' he said grimly. 'How kind you are, Mrs Forrester! But I'm afraid I'm going to decline your offer. Either we live together as husband and wife, as we did once, or you go up there and explain to your father that we are not reunited after all.'

'But how *can* we?' she retorted. 'When there's no feeling between two people it's futile, isn't it? At least this way . . .'

'You're very sure there's no feeling between the two of us, aren't you? However, I can assure you I . . .'

'Are also feeling the burden of guilt,' she interrupted starkly and stood up. 'Well, you'll just have to find some other way of getting rid of yours because the last thing I intend to become is an object of your compassion, particularly *that* way.'

'All right,' he said gently, so gently that he fooled her, but when she turned round it was to find him on his feet and the look in his grey eyes was anything but gentle.

So that she took a step backwards and said uncertainly, 'Clay . . .?'

'Don't run away, Melly,' he murmured. 'That's a coward's way out. Show me, if you can, how little you feel for me.'

She had every intention of turning and running. But then she thought suddenly that he was right—if she could stand like a stone statue and let him do his worst, he must know once and for all then . . .

The curious thing was, though, that as he slid

his arms round her the feeling that she'd thought was stone dead proved to be only dormant, that fickle feeling of warmth and security that only he could arouse in her.

How strange, she thought, to feel like this after so long. It must be an unkind trick of memory ...

But not much later, she realised what a merciless thing memory could be. She let him slide his long fingers through her hair and then wander down the slender line of her throat and although she didn't move a muscle, she found herself prey to a host of insidious recollections—enough to satisfy a drowning man ...

Clay kissing her for the first time, Clay helping her when she'd been sick on their wedding night, and telling her afterwards that he felt complimented to be compared to the Yass Show. So many Clays and the house in Darlinghurst, bright and warm on a dull, winter's afternoon. So many memories until ...

'Oh no,' she whispered despairingly, 'don't do this to me, please.'

But he did. His fingers and lips went unerringly to her tenderest most vulnerable spots, the nape of her neck, the hollows at the base of her throat, to slide down to the valley between her breasts, flicking aside the top buttons of her blouse as they went. And his other hand spread across the small of her back and curved possessively round her hips. Then he pulled her closer to him with both arms around her and bent his head to tease her lips apart with his tongue.

She resisted for all of half a minute but that was a mistake, she discovered, because he spurned her resistance like a conqueror reclaiming his own territory and began to kiss her with a savagery that hurt her at first, and surprised her in some dim recess of her mind that was still functioning, because he'd never kissed her so brutally and almost as if he was punishing her. Yet, incredibly, this treatment was drawing a response from her that didn't seem possible, and one that she couldn't hide. A response that she felt through her own body in a flood of quivering sensuousness that was as unbelievable as it was unexpected. A response that made her move in his arms and revel in the feeling of the hard length of his body against the slightness of her own, and made her offer her mouth for further punishment because it really wasn't that at all—it was something she couldn't describe . . . something . . .

She stopped trying to describe it to herself at about the same moment that Ellen appeared briefly at the drawing-room doorway, only to whisk herself away smartly and undetected but with a peculiarly satisfied look upon her face.

And when Clay lifted his head at last, she swayed in his arms and her eyes were huge and a little unfocused, and he went on holding her in his arms. 'If that's having no feeling for me, Melly,' he said, his grey gaze roaming her flushed face and parted lips, 'I can't wait to find out what you're like when you're fair-dinkum.'

She closed her eyes and felt her heart shrivel. How *could* I? she wondered bleakly. I must have gone temporarily mad!

'Melly?' he prompted.

Her eyes flew open and when she saw the look of irony on his face, they went dark and she said with an effort, 'They say when you teach a young dog a trick, he never forgets it . . .'

He laughed and she flushed vividly. 'You've got

an incredible nerve, Clay,' she said tightly. 'Not ... two nights ago, you were sleeping with someone else and now, you expect me to ... to ...' She was so angry she couldn't finish.

'Oh,' he said softly, 'so you do mind about that despite your protests to the contrary?'

'I ... it's not that I mind about it,' she flashed. 'It's just that I find it hard to fit in with your talk of a proper marriage!'

He studied her speculatively for a long time, and with a palpable air of quizzical disbelief that made her clench her teeth and say in a low intense voice, 'I *hate* you, Clay. I ...'

'Good,' he drawled. 'At least that's more truthful than what you tried to tell me before.'

'But don't you see,' she said despairingly, 'we ...'

'I see a lot, Melly,' he interrupted. 'I see that you still want me although you say you hate me— not that I mind if you prefer to call it hate for the time being. What I do mind is trying to deny its existence—by whatever name,' he said and he looked at her trembling, bruised lips and his eyes rose to hers, mockingly. 'So,' he went on coolly, 'let's have no more talk of a sham marriage because that would be adding a lie to a lie. Which is something I'm not prepared to do, sweetheart.' He released her abruptly.

'Clay ...'

'Take it or leave it, Melly,' His voice was curt. 'But you only have tonight to make up your mind.' He glanced at his watch.

'Where ... are you going somewhere?' she asked with difficulty.

'Yes. I think I'll spend the night in Yass so that you won't feel pressured if Ellen Mackenzie should show us up to the same bedroom. I'll tell her that I have some urgent business to attend to ... I'll make some excuse.'

And with those abrupt words, he left her standing there. And her hand crept up to her mouth as she heard the hired car roar down the driveway, and her eyes were tormented.

At least that's what Ellen Mackenzie thought when she found Melissa still standing in the same spot, several minutes later.

'There, there, baby,' she crooned as she folded Melissa once more into her arms. 'He'll be back, don't fret. And he's doing the right thing by you, pet. You'll see.'

Melissa stared at Ellen, her tired, confused brain not quite comprehending. 'He ... has some business,' she murmured feebly. 'Didn't he tell you?'

Ellen smiled lovingly. 'Och, he started to tell me something of the kind, but I said to him, it's not that, is it? It's because she's wound up tighter than a violin string, isn't it? And he said, yes, Nanny, she is. Take good care of her. I think he's a good man, Melissa. I know ... I know what happened, well, more or less. Your father didn't have anyone else to talk to at the time so he told me. Of course I was as angry as he was at first and for a long time. But when Mr Forrester came back to Glen Morris the second time—did you know he came down here when you ran away? Well he did and he and your father had a terrible row ... anyway, when he came back a month of so ago, I took another look at him. And I thought to myself too, that he didn't have to come back after what had been said ... the terrible, terrible things your father said to him about taking advantage of someone young and innocent, about alienating you from your family, all that and plenty more! In fact there could only have been one reason for him to come back . . . because he still cared about what had happened to you!'

'Ellen,' Melissa wept but found she couldn't go on because Ellen was the last person she'd have expected to approve of Clay.

'Oh, don't get me wrong,' Ellen persisted. 'That first time, if I'd had a gun I might have shot him. But I think he knows he did wrong and he wants to make amends. Just like your father . . . did wrong too. And it would be un-Christian not to let him.'

If she hadn't been crying, Melissa might have found that laughable. 'But don't you s-ee,' she tried to say . . .

'Yes, I saw,' Ellen interrupted pointedly. 'I saw you two hugging and a-kissing like a man and wife. Which you are. All right, maybe I'm old fashioned,' she conceded 'But I think that's sufficient reason to go back to him. After all, you did marry him, Melissa. I realise people don't hold much with the for richer and poorer, for better and worse bit these days of marriage, but _I_ hold with at least giving a body a _chance_ to make things better.'

Melissa stared at her tearfully, stunned, more confused than ever if that was possible, exasperated and frustrated. 'How . . . Daddy just assumed we were back together, Clay and I. How come you haven't?' she asked at last.

'I notice you didn't disillusion him either,' Ellen said. 'I've just been up to see him and he looks ten years younger, I vow.' She paused as if she was going to say more, to answer Melissa's question but in the end she left it at that . . .

*   *   *

'So, what's your decision, Melly?' Clay asked her the next afternoon.

It was warm and windy and the grass in the paddocks was bending in the wind and there was a smell of dust in the air.

They were on the verandah having tea, an enormous tea with two kinds of cake, scones and sandwiches which Ellen had prepared.

The wind rattled the creeper that sheltered the area where the tea-table was set and Melissa said, 'I don't seem to have much choice, do I?'

He surveyed her unsmilingly. 'That's up to you,' he said at last.

'All right,' she said in a curiously brittle voice. 'Let's be reunited. It'll be the Christian thing to do if nothing else,' she added.

His eyes narrowed. 'Another of Ellen's sayings, I presume. I didn't think you'd fooled her.'

'You have some surprising allies, Clay,' she murmured. 'Although I shouldn't be so surprised I suppose,' she went on. 'You were always renowned for your . . . winning ways with the opposite sex.'

The silence that succeeded her last remark was charged with hostility.

Then he said dryly, 'Why don't you add that you're going to hate it like hell, though? Us being reunited. And that you see yourself as some sort of martyr?'

She gasped. 'I didn't say that . . .'

'You didn't have to. It came over loud and clear anyway.'

She took a steadying breath. '*You* were the one who issued an ultimatum. And whether I like it or not, doesn't seem to mean much to you, does it? If that's left me feeling martyred . . . you might be right, Clay! I wouldn't have put it that way but you might be right. *I* would have called it feeling like the meat in the sandwich but . . .'

'Then tell your father that, Melly,' he said harshly.

'I . . . oh God!' She tried to collect her thoughts and he waited until finally, she whispered, 'I can't . . .'

There was another silence. Until he said abruptly, 'All right. Let's get this show on the road. I've spoken to his doctors again and they want to move him to Sydney as soon as possible.'

CHAPTER SEVEN

THE next few days passed in a blur of activity.

James Heatley was moved to a private Sydney clinic and Melissa and Clay, ironically, took up residence in the penthouse suite of his hotel because it was handy to the clinic. Ellen Mackenzie accompanied them and was accommodated in a suite of rooms next door. And it became evident after only a few hours in residence that that dour, Scots lady was going to have much pleasure interfering with the staff of the hotel whenever she could and if the accent on service to a guests every whim had not been firmly engrained in said staff, it wasn't hard to imagine what kind of a situation could have arisen.

In fact it was Ellen who provided Melissa with the only source of amusement that came her way during those few days.

And it came the day after they'd moved into the hotel. A delicious lunch had been sent up for Melissa which Ellen had returned saying it was far too fancy and what Melissa needed was some good, plain food that was well cooked. In fact she'd not only returned it but descended to the kitchen herself, with it, to describe to the Italian chef exactly what she meant by good, plain food.

The ensuing mêlée had been described to Melissa by the hotel manager, who fortunately possessed a sense of humour, and had been able to intervene when Ellen had demanded a beef stew with vegetables and no foreign muck in it at all—

thereby deeply wounding the chef's Latin sensibilities.

So it was that Clay found Melissa smiling to herself after she'd eaten enough stew to fatten an ox and been told to take a nap. Ellen herself had retired to do likewise.

'What is it?'

Melissa turned with a start. She hadn't heard him arrive—he'd gone to work early and she'd assumed he'd be away all day. And the smile faltered and died.

'Oh, nothing really,' she said quietly and turned away again as he loosened his tie and slung his jacket over the back of a chair.

He walked over to her and turned her back with his hands on her shoulders. 'Melissa,' he said and her eyes flew to his because he never called her that, 'it's no good shutting me out like this. We're not going to achieve anything this way beyond making it even harder for you.'

'I can't help it if . . .'

'Yes you can,' he said roughly. 'For better or for worse, there's no way out of this situation and it's only being ridiculous for us to act like strangers. Ridiculous if for no other reason than that we're *not*. Besides, so far I'm only asking you to talk to me. I haven't forced you to share my bed.' His eyes mocked her.

'Would you force me, Clay?' she said huskily.

'I don't suppose I'd have to after the way you kissed me back a few days ago,' he said brutally. 'But I've no doubt you're going to hate yourself when it happens, however it happens—especially if it happens willingly,' he said sarcastically.

She went white. 'It won't,' she said in a fierce undertone.

'We'll see,' he remarked with a look of cynicism that made her long to hit out at him but she resisted the impulse and pulled away from him instead.

He let her go but said, 'Why were you smiling just now?' And there was an underlying note in his voice that warned her of his impatience.

She took a deep breath. *'All right,'* she said not quite steadily. 'It was Ellen.' She told him what had happened.

'My God!' he said with a faint grin. 'She obviously has no idea how sought after Nino is by every major restaurant in Sydney—and Melbourne and Adelaide and Perth for that matter. And how much it costs to retain his services here,' he added significantly.

'She's like that,' Melissa said candidly. 'She's the kind of person who rushes in where angels fear to tread. She's also,' she stopped because the words were slipping out quite naturally and that surprised her, 'she's also,' she went on more slowly, 'treating me as if I was twelve, a victim of a concentration camp, and someone she's afraid to let out of her sight in case I run away again.'

He ignored her last words and looked her over consideringly. 'You are thin,' he murmured.

'Not really. At least I don't think so. I was never fat.'

'No.' He shrugged and his eyes glinted suddenly. 'You were beautifully slender if I recall with some astonishingly lovely curves—you reminded me of a delicate porcelain figurine.'

Melissa felt a faint heat come to her cheeks but she refused to allow herself to be intimidated by it. 'Well I'm sorry if I'm no longer . . . that way,' she said dryly. 'Perhaps Ellen's efforts to fatten me up will render me more to your taste,' she added sarcastically. 'Not that I care one way or the other, but I suppose that now Mrs Clayton Forrester is to be exposed to the public you'd like her to at least look worthy of you.' She stared at him coolly.

He took his time about replying and in the meantime matched her cool look with one of his own. Then he drawled, 'I was right—I don't think I like the way you've grown up, Melissa. You used to be the least bitchy girl I knew.'

'Has it never occurred to you that you expect an awful lot of me, Clay?' she said tightly.

'Do I?' His eyes were suddenly sombre. He shrugged. 'Perhaps,' he murmured. 'But then is it a lot to expect?'

'*Yes,*' she spat at him, suddenly incensed. 'It is!'

'What is?' he shot back at her. 'Too much to expect that we can conduct a civilised conversation?'

'Your idea of a civilised conversation is much too personal for me, I'm afraid,' she flung at him. 'If I have to go through with this, the last thing I want to be reminded of is what or how I was like before. If you must know, I *hate* how I was before. I *hate* being reminded that I was so naive that you could plot and plan to marry me without me even realising what was going on. So don't think you're doing me a favour by dragging all that up.'

'All right,' he said through his teeth and his grey gaze raked her mercilessly, 'we'll bury Melly Heatley who became Melly Forrester, who more than a little found her way into Clayton Forrester's heart. We'll write her off as if she never existed—and I'm beginning to doubt that she did, and we'll concentrate on *Melissa,* someone I don't know a great deal about but could be persuaded to learn to know *provided*,' he said the word with a sort of deadly menace, 'she doesn't forget some things. That I don't have to carry on this marriage if you're so bloody dead set against it and me, Melissa. And I certainly don't have to be a tame, lap dog kind of a husband that you can treat like yesterday's newspaper—in fact I must warn you I'm just as liable to put you over my knee and spank some sense into you instead. And last but not least, in case you've forgotten, it's *your* father who is to be the benificiary of this marriage. Your father, who you couldn't tell the truth to—if you know the truth, Melissa.'

'The truth being, I presume,' she said flatly, 'that I never fell out of love with you, Clay? Is that what you're going to set out to prove?' She laughed hollowly. 'You're welcome to try,' she added calmly, 'if you enjoy banging your head against a brick wall.'

But some of her calm deserted her as his lips tightened and a look of cold anger came into his eyes. She moved away a step, involuntarily, and all of a sudden his lips twisted and he smiled, a lethal kind of smile that frightened her even more than the anger had.

'What is it?' he queried. 'Afraid I'll be tempted to ... bang my head against a brick wall only to find it's made of straw? Like the night at Glen Morris?' he added gently.

'Oh ...' she breathed, so angry it was all she could do not to faint from rage. Then she twisted around and ran across the elegant lounge to the door of the bedroom she used, slamming the door behind her and locking it. She flung herself on the bed and pounded the pillow with her fists, crying with great gulping sobs as she'd never cried in her life before.

But it did her little good because for the first time in a long time, she began to feel sick for no real reason—and was.

So much for Ellen's good, plain, fattening beef stew, procured so dramatically, she thought bitterly, when it was over. She closed her eyes wearily, then made herself take a shower and lay down on the bed in her light cotton wrapper and stared up at the ceiling with stark, bemused eyes.

'I can't go on like this . . .'

The words escaped without her realising she was talking to herself. But once said, they seemed to release some inner floodgates of thought, and for the first time since she'd knocked on Tanya Miller's door, she found herself thinking deeply and probingly, and not so much of the past as of the present . . .

And presently she thought, he's right. I've been carrying on ridiculously. I got myself back into this marriage because of my father and the only thing to do is try to make the best of it. And I suppose, if I'm going to be honest, the reason I've been acting like a real little bitch, is because when he kissed me and I reacted the way I did, I felt as if I'd betrayed myself somehow. I was so sure he wouldn't be able to make me feel that way again . . .

And even today, she mused and moved restlessly, if anyone had told me that I'd feel hurt because he no longer calls me Melly, that for him Melly Heatley is buried, I'd have said no, no I'm not hurt, in fact I'll drink to that! Let's bury her well and truly. But instead it . . . hurt.

So what does it all mean? she asked herself.

Perhaps there is some truth in what I said about teaching young dogs tricks. Maybe some habits are hard to shake ... when you're in such close contact with someone you've known so well?

But that answer didn't seem to satisfy her. In fact there seemed to be only one solution and that was to take her life from now on day by day, hour by hour, not in thoughtless emotion some of which sprang from hidden roots within her which she couldn't decipher, but as someone who was mature enough to accept fate and circumstance and live with it.

She closed her eyes wearily. Easier said than done, she thought. But I just don't have a choice, do I?

'Clay,' she said the next morning over breakfast.

He looked up, his eyes faintly narrowed as if he'd detected something in her voice that he wasn't expecting.

She looked away briefly. 'I ... I'm sorry I've been so ...' She grimaced and contemplated her breakfast plate. 'Well, I'm sorry,' she went on a little indistinctly.

He didn't say anything and finally she looked up and looked directly into those probingly acute grey eyes. 'I was being childish,' she added huskily.

He didn't agree or disagree, merely said, 'You've had a few shocks over the past few days, Melissa.'

She winced inwardly but forced herself to go on. 'What I wanted to say was that I do appreciate what you're doing for my father, and for me, and I won't be making it,' she swallowed, 'difficult from now on. And ...'

'Go on,' he murmured.

'Well, I wondered what kind of life you ... we

were going to lead now . . .' She stopped uncertainly.

He stretched out a hand and picked up the silver salt cellar and twirled it in his long fingers. 'The quieter the better I think,' he said slowly, 'until the operation is over, anyway. Did you think I was going to plunge you into a madly social whirl?'

'No,' she said awkwardly. 'But I don't want you to feel—stifled.'

He shrugged. 'Thank you for your concern but if this is getting back to what you said about me going my own way . . .'

'It's not that,' she interrupted hastily and changed tack deliberately. 'It . . . won't be a secret anymore, will it? Our marriage, I mean.'

'No.'

'I wonder what people will think?' she mused.

'They can think what they like,' he said flatly. 'But if you're worried that someone is going to dig up the fact that we were married three years ago and separated for most of the time, I don't think you need be. Very few people knew. In fact just about the only person who knew about it in an unprofessional, non-family capacity was Tiffany Evans.

Melissa started. 'Tiffany. Is she in Sydney?'

'No. She's overseas at present.'

Melissa looked at him questioningly. 'We kept in touch,' he said briefly and added, 'the others in the know like the various agencies that searched for you so unsuccessfully have been well paid for their discretion. So I don't think you need to worry about becoming the object of all the gossip columns.'

'I hadn't even thought of that,' she said quietly and blinked away a tear because it was even harder than she'd expected it would be to get through to him.

'May I ask you a question?' he said abruptly.

She nodded.

'This ... I presume this is a kind of amnesty you're offering, does it extend to us resuming physical relations, Melissa?' His eyes were pure grey and seemed to pierce her very soul. 'Because that's the one thing that will make it easier for us.'

'I ...' she whispered and felt the heat pour into her face so that she put her hands to her cheeks in an involuntary gesture that was as foolish as it was futile.

'I thought not,' he said finally and stood up.

'No—Clay,' she stammered and stood up herself. 'Please ...'

'Please what, Melissa?'

'Just give me a little time,' she whispered.

They stared at each other for an age. Grey eyes into lavender-blue ones and there was tension stamped into every line of his tall figure, and she herself felt as if her breathing had been suspended.

Then he relaxed visibly. 'Very well,' he said. 'If that's what you want.' His voice was even and she thought she must have imagined the fleeting look of relief she saw in his eyes. Why should there be relief? she wondered. It must have been something else.

She pressed her hands together and tried to think of something light and inconsequential to say, to end the awkwardness of the moment. But just then Ellen knocked and entered the suite rather like a battleship in full steam, and Clay looked at her ruefully and the moment was past.

A month after her conversation with Clay over

breakfast, Melissa looked back and couldn't believe how time had passed or how she'd settled into a routine that had once been impossible to even contemplate.

She spent a lot of time each day at the clinic with her father, where the specialists he was under had decided to get him as physically fit as was possible before embarking on what was major surgery.

Melissa had an interview with one of the doctors attending him and he outlined for her very honestly that even with the new technique her father still only had a fifty-fifty chance of survival. Then he went on to say, 'One positive thing in your father's favour, Mrs Forrester, is his great will to live. Now,' he toyed with his pen and then looked at her directly, 'don't let me delude you— that is often not enough. Sometimes the odds are just too great. However, I tend not to discount it either. Please,' he added gently, 'I'm not saying this to buoy your hopes up unfairly. But he does have that. And in the last resort, even while he's fighting so hard, he seems to have an air of peace and achievement about him. I'm not a fanciful man, Mrs Forrester, but I try not to be only a technician. He's happy, isn't he?' He looked at her questioningly.

'Yes . . .' Melissa closed her eyes but the tears squeezed through.

'Is there something you'd like to tell me, Mrs Forrester?' the doctor said after a pause.

'No—well, only that it seems crazy for this to have had to happen for me to be able to work things out. I . . . I fell out with my father a few years ago with, I thought, very good cause. But now it seems . . .'

She stopped speaking and wiped her eyes with the back of her hand, and shrugged.

'The prospect of death,' the doctor said quietly, 'does that, I've observed. It makes us realise how petty and trivial we can be at times. All of us,' he added significantly. 'So you mustn't think you're alone in this. We all do things we regret. But you've achieved something many people don't get the chance to. You've achieved a reconciliation and peace and happiness for your father.'

'Yes,' she said raggedly. 'Yes . . .'

But she thought of the doctor's words many times over the next few weeks and each time with a growing sense of discomfort. Because what he hadn't known and what her father didn't know, was that she was cheating in the sense that a lot of the peace and happiness she'd achieved for her father was based on a lie.

Another aspect of what the doctor had said bothered her too. The bit about being petty and trivial. Because if that had been proved in her father's case, might not it also apply to Clay?

Was it petty and trivial to run away from them *both*, in other words? she reflected one evening with an inward sigh and looked across the lamplit room to where Clay was reading the paper. It was a hot night and the French windows that led on to the roof garden were wide open.

In fact the roof garden had provided her with something of a hobby during those weeks. She'd been drawn to it like a magnet not long after arriving from Glen Morris and had persuaded the hotel manager to let her take care of it, apart from the real grass which had to be mowed. And she'd derived solace and comfort from tending the plants, pruning and watering, digging in the real soil, adding to the pot-plants, and often just sitting high above Sydney surrounded by the fragrance of the lemon trees in tubs, and the roses.

And she'd definitely needed something to provide some solace from the strain of worrying about her father, and the strain of living with Clay again.

Not that she saw a great deal of Clay. He spent a good deal of time at his office and often brought work home with him at night. But most nights he went to see her father with her and it was not that he did anything or said anything to upset her, in fact it was as if he was deliberately steering clear of any emotional issues and she realised this and was grateful. So the strain didn't lie there, she reasoned that hot night, and tried to put her finger on exactly where it did lie. And could only come to the conclusion that it was a host of little things about living with him that made her feel tense and on edge. Because so many of them reminded her remorselessly of the first two months of her marriage, the little things she'd loved as much as . . .

She cut her thoughts off deliberately and her gaze came back and she flushed faintly as she realised he'd lifted his head from the paper and was watching her.

'I . . . I think I'll go to bed,' she said quietly and stood up.

But once in bed those thoughts she'd cut off came back to plague her. All the little things about Clay that reminded her so vividly of those days . . . Like the day before when she'd been just about to step into the shower and she'd heard the main door of the suite open and close and the unmistakable sound of Clay dropping his briefcase.

And she'd trembled suddenly and recalled with the utmost clarity the day, after they'd been married about a month, when he'd come and found her in the shower and stepped in with her, clothes and all.

'You're mad!' she'd said, laughing helplessly all the same.

'Mmm,' he'd replied, taking her glistening, wet body into his arms. 'Mad about you . . .'

And as she lay in the darkness, she bit her lip and couldn't help remembering what had followed that incident in the shower—the lovemaking—and she turned her head into the pillow and clenched her fists to make it go away.

But it wasn't only those kind of thoughts she found herself battling with. More and more she couldn't help wondering how Clay had spent the last three years. Had he slipped back into his old lifestyle—into a succession of worldly, elegant mistresses . . . like Tanya?

'I think he must have,' she murmured to herself one day. 'Even if I was wrong about what I saw the day I ran away . . . I mean, look what he was doing when I met him again. I know—I know what Tanya said about it, all the same, I'm sure there must have been other women. I think she might have got that bit wrong, about him not having had any warmth . . . Not the kind of women he'd take to the zoo though, and not the kind who would foolishly and naively imagine Clayton Forrester would be content to live in a little house and . . . What a fool I was,' she mused. 'And more of a hick than I realised not to even wonder about that. But then aren't I being a fool now? To be wondering about the women in his life after I left . . .'

All the same, no amount of telling herself that she was a fool, and no amount of adding a rider like, why shouldn't he have had a succession of mistresses, anyway, quite stopped her from thinking and wondering about it. And even picturing him with another woman in his arms, and feeling a curious jolt of her heart at the same time.

Which is . . . strange, she told herself once. Not to think of him for so long and now this . . .

But the strangest thing of all, she often thought, was his insistence that they make this a proper marriage. He must *know*, she reflected, that you can't do that when two people don't love each other. It must be guilt . . .

Five weeks after their arrival in Sydney the doctors set a date for the operation. It was to be in a week's time and when Melissa had been advised of it, after visiting her father one day, she did what she often did at the clinic, slipped down to the nursery to see the babies through the observation window. She knew it was something she shouldn't do to herself and in fact, the first time it had happened, it had been by accident. She'd got out of the lift on the wrong floor which had turned out to be the maternity floor, and wandered down the corridor to come upon the nursery. After that day, it had drawn her like a magnet, something she couldn't resist even though every time she watched those tiny scraps of humanity it was like feeling a knife twist in her heart.

But this day, Clay found her there.

She looked her fill and forced herself to turn away, only to look straight up into his grey eyes.

'. . . Clay?' she said unsteadily, and licked her

lips. 'How . . . I mean why . . . is something wrong? My father?'

'No,' he said slowly, and there was something puzzled and sombre in the way his eyes searched her face.

'Then what are you doing here?' she heard herself saying rapidly. 'And how did you find me?' She tried to make her voice light.

'The sister on your father's floor,' he said at last. 'She told me I'd only missed you by a couple of minutes and suggested I try here because she suspected that the nursery held more than a little attraction for you. She saw you here once.'

'Did she? Sprung!' Melissa said with a grin. 'Yes it does, I have to confess. They're so sweet, aren't they? Well, some of them look like little old men and so cross! And others seem to be able to sleep through anything. Like that one over there.' She pointed towards a crib and went on without a tremor in her voice, 'I've never had much to do with a new baby. They're a real novelty to me, that's why I'm a bit fascinated I guess.'

He stared at her wordlessly for so long, her heart began to hammer uncomfortably. But finally he half smiled and shrugged at the same time and said something about babies making a lot of noise, and she relaxed and even congratulated herself on her acting ability. And it was only later that she seriously questioned why she was so determined that Clay should never find out about the baby she'd lost. But she didn't come up with an answer—at least not one that satisfied her.

But as the day of the operation grew nearer she forgot about most other things. And then it dawned and she watched her father being wheeled away.

The hours that followed seemed like a lifetime and the delicate, tricky operation went over schedule and Melissa's heart sank as the time ticked by and she was convinced of the worst. But finally he was wheeled out of surgery and the surgeons were expressing guarded optimism but said a lot hinged on the next few hours. Major surgery was in itself a shock, they said.

For nearly twenty-four hours Melissa scarcely left his bedside. Then the doctors pronounced him out of danger although it was still too soon to comment on the success of the operation, they said, and Clay made her go home with him. Ellen took over the vigil and added her weight to Clay's.

Melissa was white with tiredness and strain when they got up to the penthouse suite and she just stood in the middle of the lounge as Clay switched on the lamps and rang for room service.

Then he took her by the hand and led her to the settee and sat her down on it. He bent down to take her shoes off and curled her legs up on the settee, and pulled some cushions behind her head. 'We'll have something to eat,' he said quietly. 'You look as if you need it.'

'I don't think I could eat,' she murmured.

'You must,' he answered.

When the meal arrived he wheeled the trolley over to her and sat down beside her. He handed her a napkin and dished her up a small portion of deliciously fragrant Osso Bucco, a veal dish for which Chef Nino was renowned in Sydney. There was a dressed green salad to go with it and a bottle of Sauterne.

She took the plate and watched Clay pour the golden wine into two tall glasses.

'Have a sip first,' he offered and handed her the

glass. She did and the taste as well as the label told her it was one of the finest sauternes, that relied for its sweetness on the grape and nothing added, so it wasn't cloying. She put the glass down and began to eat. And to her surprise, ate it all. Then she laid her head back on the cushions and drained her glass. 'I know how to cook Osso Bucco,' she said almost dreamily. 'Perhaps I should compare notes with Mr Nino?'

'I'm sure he'd be delighted,' Clay said gravely and poured her some more wine.

She sipped it and grinned. 'I doubt that. I mean, that he'd be delighted. Whenever we meet he gives me a really strange look because I'm the person who is indirectly responsible for the odd dishes Ellen commands him to bend his talents to.'

'He may think they're odd but it seems Ellen is a sound nutritionist.' He looked at her significantly.

She wrinkled her nose. 'I know! I'm putting on weight but her kind of food gets a bit boring sometimes. Did you know she'd even taken food over to my father . . .' She stopped abruptly and her face crumpled. 'Oh Clay,' she said brokenly, 'I thought he was going to die . . .'

'I know,' he said gently and as if it was the most natural thing in the world, reached over to take her in his arms.

She wept into his shoulder unrestrainedly and he stroked her hair and held her close. And that same feeling of warmth and security began to steal over her as it had done that night at Glen Morris so that her sobs diminished and finally, she pulled away a little and looked up at him, her eyes violet in the lamplight, and wondering, and tormented.

'What is it?' he said softly.

She hesitated. '. . . It's you,' she said at last with a painful sort of honesty.

He stared down at her frowningly and she tried to look away after a while but found she couldn't. It was as if she was held captive by his eyes but not only that, by everything that was Clayton Forrester. The clever lines of his face, the way his hair, now threaded with silver still fell a little over his forehead, those lines that were permanently beside his mouth, the bulk of him beneath his light grey suit that she couldn't help thinking about . . .

She knew it so well, she thought with a pang. The smooth powerful line of his shoulders, the narrowing torso and the long strong legs. The body that had had the power to subdue hers, crush her, but never had until the night he'd kissed her at Glen Morris. And even that had had about it a heady kind of defeat that hadn't really tasted of defeat.

No, she thought. He was always gentle with me in bed. And it was so lovely, it was like nothing else I can think of. He made me feel like a princess. He made me feel special, sometimes witty, sometimes rather daring, other times a little dumb but glad to be so that he could teach me, and all the time . . . Melly, a person who only existed for him . . .

Do I want all that again, she thought with some despair, as if nothing ever came between us? How *could* I?

'Melissa?'

She started.

'Have you had enough time—is that what you're trying to tell me?' His lips barely moved but his words sent something like an electric shock through her body.

'I ...' her voice quivered, 'I don't know ... I
...' she stammered. And something inside her
seemed to be engaged in a terrible conflict. So that
finally she whispered anguishedly, 'Yes. But I
don't know *why*. It might be just because I need
some comfort. Tanya said,' she flushed but went
on resolutely, 'that's all it means sometimes.'

Clay's mouth twisted. 'Tanya's very wise,
sometimes. But if she said that in the context I
think she might have, it could be like applying her
wisdom like a plaster to the wrong situation. You
... confided a fair bit in Tanya, didn't you?' he
added, taking her by surprise.

'A little,' she said shakily. 'Why? Does that have
something to do with ... this?'

'Not directly, no,' he said dryly. 'But,' he
searched her face with narrowed eyes, 'if you only
want to go to bed with me for ... comfort, let's
leave it.' And he released her and laid her back
against the cushions.

Melissa's eyes widened. 'I thought you wanted it
... us ...' She broke off uncertainly.

He picked up his wine glass and drained it. 'I
did.' His eyes were on the glass in his hands. Then
he turned his head to look at her. 'But not like
this, and I'll tell you why. One of your main
grievances against me, I think, is that I set out to
make you fall in love with me—in more practical,
less pretty words—that I seduced you.'

She caught her breath and started to speak but
he overrode her, quietly yet implacably. 'It's the
same thing, Melissa.'

'I ...'

'It has to be.' His mouth was suddenly pale.
'Otherwise why would you have taken such drastic
action? That's what you thought, isn't it?' His eyes

were bleak and she twisted her head away but he forced her to look back at him with his fingers under her chin. 'Why don't you admit it?' he queried harshly. 'Because if that wasn't what you thought, why did you run away?'

She trembled and bit her lip and her eyes were suddenly agonised. And when she framed her lips to say the word he sought, she had a terribly hollow feeling that she wasn't telling the truth, at least not the whole truth. But she said in a low husky voice. 'Yes.'

'Right,' his voice was still harsh, 'then you must see that the last thing I'm going to do, this time round, is give you any cause to believe that I've seduced you again. This time round when we make love, if we make love, it will only be when you admit to yourself that you really want it, that you want me, not comfort or consolation or anything else.'

She took a breath and her face was very pale as she sat up suddenly. 'All right, Clay.' Her voice was not quite steady but her eyes never left his. 'If this is what you want to hear, I'll tell you. I do want you. I never thought it would be like this again but I was wrong. Now ... now that I'm back with you, it seems I can't forget the way you used to make love to me, and I want that again. What I don't want is for it to go under the wrong *name*. You see, when I'm away from you ... well, for over two years I didn't even think of you. It's only when I'm with you!' She moved her hands and looked away briefly and when she looked back his lips were set tight, and she thought with a jolt of her heart, that he was coldly angry. But it didn't stop her from going on.

'You don't like to hear that, do you, Clay? But

it shouldn't surprise you. You wanted me once when you didn't love me. And I should imagine you've wanted ... other women over the past three years in the same way, and they've wanted you. Oh, it's not that I'm condemning you, please don't think that. But the difference is that we've ... sort of been forced into a situation where we've got to pretend it's *more* than that when it's not. I ... I appreciate you wanting to do that for me, I really do but,' she shrugged, tiredly, 'it doesn't alter the fact that ...'

'Doesn't alter the fact,' he interrupted very quietly, 'that I was more right than I knew when I said you would hate yourself if you ever let me take you to bed? That's really what it all means ... what you've been trying to say but in a more polite fashion?'

'Yes,' she whispered.

'I see,' he said finally and stood up. 'I think you should get some sleep now.'

She stared up at him. 'Clay ...'

'No, leave it, Melissa,' he said abruptly. 'You've told me all I wanted to know, or almost all. Come, you must be exhausted. Goodnight, my dear ...'

CHAPTER EIGHT

A GREY, overcast dawn greeted Melissa's eyes the next morning.

She'd slept well, at least heavily, which was the last thing she'd expected, but her body must have taken over. The only thing was, as one often does after a very heavy sleep, she felt lethargic physically and overburdened mentally, although that might not have been caused by the quality of sleep.

No, she thought with a deep sigh and reached for a pillow to hug in her arms. That comes from what happened last night . . .

She buried her face in the pillow and remembered with a deadly kind of clarity, everything she'd said to Clay, and felt again that kind of hollow feeling at the pit of her stomach as she wondered again if she'd been honest with herself, let alone him. Yet the facts seemed to speak for themselves. She *couldn't* square with her conscience what was happening to her now. Who could? she wondered miserably. To want to go back to how they were was like saying, all right, I don't mind what you did, I enjoyed it anyway, and perhaps I was being petty and trivial to be so . . . devastated. Oh God! But *was* I?

She lifted her face wearily from the pillow and stared across the room bleakly. Then her bedside phone rang.

It was Ellen and Melissa remembered her father with a jolt. 'How is he?' she asked nervously.

Ellen spoke at length but the gist of it was that

he'd had a good night and was awake and lucid and looking forward to seeing Melissa.

'I'll be right there . . .'

Ellen snorted down the wire. 'You will not,' she said strongly. 'You'll take time to have a proper breakfast which I'll order for you now. Put me back to the switchboard,' she commanded.

Melissa did as she was bid with a sigh.

She chose her clothes carefully from her new wardrobe, settling for a summery, primrose yellow culotte suit which she wore with a black silk top that had tiny yellow flowers on it and low-heeled black patent leather shoes. Since coming to Sydney she'd had her hair cut quite short but so that it looked and fell naturally as only a first-class haircut can.

She stared into the mirror when she had finished dressing, a thing she'd got out of the habit of doing too searchingly. But the grave face with faintly shadowed eyes that stared back at her, told her only one thing, that despite Ellen's attempts to feed her up, and despite the fact that she was no longer quite painfully thin, there was no resemblance between this girl—and Melly Forrester, that she could see.

She turned away impatiently and opened her jewel box to select a long gold chain and matching bracelet to go with her outfit. But after she'd put the chain on, she stood fingering it for a while, lost in thought.

When she'd taken flight nearly three years ago, all she'd taken with her had been the most basic wardrobe, a framed photo of her mother, a few papers like her birth certificate, and by accident her marriage certificate. The only other thing she'd taken, apart from her own savings, had been her wedding ring and she hadn't been able to understand why she'd taken that. But the thing she'd most deliberately left behind, had been her jewel box which had contained a small fortune.

Her engagement ring for one thing, a pale blue sapphire from Ceylon set in a circle of diamonds, the diamond-studded bracelet her father had given her on her eighteenth birthday and a selection of her mother's jewellery like the solid gold chain she was wearing now—a collection whose worth would have probably fed her for years.

But she'd left if all behind in a repulsion of spirit, thinking in her shock and misery that she hadn't wanted to be tainted by anything to do with James Heatley who had caused so much misery in so many lives, or ever be reminded of the way Clay had retaliated, let alone live off the profits of anything bestowed on her by either of them.

And her jewel box was the only thing Clay had apparently kept of her personal belongings. He'd produced it a few days after they'd arrived in Sydney but had said nothing.

And she'd worn the diamond bracelet and seen her father's tired face light up, but she hadn't ever worn her engagement ring. And a strange thought slid across her mind as she stared down at the sapphire ring lying in its bed of peach velvet—to forgive one but not the other, is that fair and reasonable? Then she realised almost immediately that it wasn't such a strange thought in that its sentiments had been plaguing her for some time. But it's not that I haven't *forgiven* Clay ... or is it?

A discreet knock on the suite door brought her out of her tangled thoughts.

It was her breakfast, delivered personally as it was every morning, by the hotel manager.

'Thank you, Mr Jackson,' Melissa said and smiled at him as he wheeled the trolley over to the French windows and placed a chair for her. 'It's very kind of you to take the trouble every morning. I suppose Mr Forrester . . .' She stopped a little uncomfortably, because it seemed strange to admit that she had no idea whether Clay had gone or not. She glanced at his closed bedroom door and flushed faintly.

'Not at all, Mrs Forrester,' Mr Jackson said and if he noticed her discomfort, gave no sign of it. 'You are after all, our most special guest. By the way,' he added with a twinkle in his eye, 'seeing as Miss Mackenzie is not here this morning, I took the liberty of omitting the oatmeal she ordered for you. I . . . er . . . once detected from your expression that you weren't a great fan of oatmeal porridge.'

'How right you are,' Melissa said with a grin. 'I wish I had the courage to tell her that, though!'

'Miss Mackenzie is a very formidable lady,' he said understandingly. 'Oh, by the way again, Mr Forrester asked me to tell you that something unexpected has come up in Melbourne which necessitated him flying down for the day. But he said he'd be back by this evening and that he didn't want to disturb you this morning. He left quite early.'

Melissa smiled again, but a little mechanically this time and when she was on her own, she stared unseeingly through the French windows and for no reason at all, felt a flicker of apprehension touch her, no reason that she could put her finger on at least. Except, that thinking back over the past few days and last night particularly, made her realise that Clay had been different lately. Especially last night, although all she could describe it as, was a kind of reserve, a new, different kind of reserve about him. But how that could possibly tie up with a business trip to Melbourne, she pondered, is beyond me. I must be imagining things . . .

But that feeling of apprehension stayed with her through the morning even in face of the tremendous news she got from the doctors. It seemed they were now willing to pronounce the operation a complete success and go even further, predict many more healthy years for her father.

'Oh, Daddy,' she whispered with tears in her eyes when she saw him, 'I'm so happy for you . . .'

'Melissa, Melissa,' he said with tears in his own eyes, 'without you, I didn't even want to live. But you came back to me . . .'

'I should never have gone away from you,' she said shakenly. 'I'll never do it again.'

He started to say something but stopped and drew her weakly into his arms instead. But she had the feeling with a tightening of her heart, that he'd been going to say something about Clay, and that too added to the insidious load of apprehension she seemed to be carrying.

Yet when he spoke again it was about Ellen, not Clay, and nothing of much consequence, just something they laughed over and were still smiling about when that good lady appeared, to demand what the joke was . . .

I should be feeling on top of the world, Melissa thought when she got back to the penthouse that afternoon. But I'm *not*. I feel as nervous and jumpy as a cat on hot tiles and about as confused as . . .

'Oh damn,' she muttered out aloud and kicked off her shoes and reached for the phone to order some tea.

And when the knock came on the door, she called out tiredly, 'Come in. It's open.' And turned expecting to see a white-jacketed waiter with a trolley but instead it was Tiffany Evans who stood in the doorway, clinging to the doorknob as if it was the only thing that was stopping her from falling.

'*Melissa*,' she whispered. 'Am I dreaming?'

'Tiffany . . . oh, Tiffany!'

Then they were in each other's arms laughing and crying at the same time and tea arrived in the middle of it all to add to the confusion.

But finally some sanity prevailed and Melissa poured the tea and Tiffany sat back with her cup and saucer.

'Do I need this!' she said feelingly. 'You haven't got a tot of rum to put in it by any chance? No, I'm only joking. But tell me, what brought about this miracle?' she added plaintively.

Melissa took a breath. 'I . . . I was in Melbourne and I ran into Clay one day. It was the most amazing coincidence,' she said lightly.

'And now you're back together,' Tiffany said wonderingly. Then her eyes narrowed when Melissa didn't reply, just nodded after a barely perceptible hesitation.

'Clay,' Tiffany said tentatively then, 'was out of his mind with worry when you left. We all were.'

Melissa lifted her eyes from their rather unseeing contemplation of her tea-cup. 'It was a very ... ill-judged thing to do,' she said miserably. 'I'm sorry.' She looked down again.

'He told me what had happened—how it had happened.'

Melissa looked up swiftly.

'He told me,' Tiffany said quietly, 'because I accused him of playing fast and loose with you and I said that if you got in touch with me, the last thing I'd do would be to let him know. I was a little distraught, I'm afraid. But even so, I couldn't mistake the desperation about him.'

'He,' Melissa said with an effort, 'like everyone else, thought I was still a child ...'

'Well,' Tiffany said slowly, 'that's what I told myself too. But I changed my mind ... Melissa, what is this?' she said straightly. '*Are* you back with him?' She looked around and then at Melissa's unhappy face. '*Tell* me,' she said compellingly, 'don't shut me out this time. What's the good of having friends if you don't use them!' There was no doubting the genuine note of anguish in her voice.

'Oh Tiff,' Melissa said with tears streaming down her face. 'I'm sorry, you were the best friend I ever had. All right, I'll tell you.' She did, about her father's illness, everything that had happened since the day she'd knocked on Tanya Miller's door although she made no mention of Tanya or those circumstances. 'But you see,' she concluded, 'nothing's changed really ... except me. I mean Clay wants to do the decent, the right thing but ...'

'What do you mean, except you?' Tiffany shot at her.

Melissa hesitated miserably. 'I ... realised it was only a crush I had on him and that I've grown up, grown out of it, whatever.'

'You don't sound very sure of that. Why don't you try to convince me?' Tiffany said quietly.

Melissa was silent for a long time. Then she said huskily, 'Tiff ... it's one thing to be attracted to Clay. I think we both agreed long ago, how easy that is ... well,' she shrugged, 'I mean ...'

'Oh, I know what you mean. We agreed he was gorgeous and all the rest of it,' Tiffany said ironically. 'So that's all it was?' she went on conversationally. 'You know, you could have fooled me. I could have sworn it was more than that. I could have sworn that you fell so deeply in love with Clay that what happened hurt you so very badly, you had to run away from it.'

'Do you honestly think I should have stayed?' Melissa cried.

'Yes.'

'Tiffany ...'

'Melissa—all right,' Tiffany said. 'It's very easy to speak with the benefit of hindsight. I'm sorry but perhaps I'm a bit more qualified to comment on it than you might imagine. And perhaps it's what you need to hear,' she added significantly. 'Then you might ... rethink your own ... mind, on the subject.'

'I don't think I know what you're talking about,' Melissa said wearily. 'What is there to rethink? *You* tell me what has changed. Don't forget Clay told me why he married me. And you were the one who told me how different I was to the other woman he'd had in his life. I mean it all added up so perfectly once I realised ... And do you think I don't know that there must have been other women over the past three years? So what can have changed?'

'There've been no other women over the past

three years, Melissa.'

'Tiffany,' Melissa said distraughtly, 'only about six weeks ago . . .' She stopped abruptly and took a confused breath. And realised for the first time that although she wanted to believe what Tanya had said, although she didn't actually disbelieve it from Tanya's point of view and liked her, it *hurt* to think of Clay with her . . .

Hurt so much in fact, Tiffany must have seen it in her eyes because she sat forward and said with a deadly kind of intent, 'If it worries you, if you can't stand to think of Clay with another woman, ask yourself *why* one day. But in the meantime, let me explain to you what I was trying to say about hindsight earlier.' She breathed deeply. 'After you ran away, I don't think I've hated anyone as I thought I hated Clay. I'd always had my doubts about him, you see, and on top of it, I felt as guilty as hell. I felt that there must have been something I could have done to stop you marrying him. So, it became like a personal vendetta. After that first scene I got in touch with him and apologised and told him I'd do all I could to help. And I kept in touch with him frequently, in fact I did more than that . . . a lot more than that,' she said grimly. 'I kept tabs on him.'

Melissa blinked. 'How?' she whispered. 'Why?'

'Why? Because, as I said I couldn't doubt his desperation. But I didn't think it would last and I felt I had a personal stake in getting to the bottom of Clayton Forrester. I thought he'd tire of his feelings of remorse or whatever they were pretty quickly and then I'd be able to have the vicious satisfaction of exposing him to himself for what he really was—someone you'd be better off without . . .'

Melissa looked at her wordlessly.

'But as the months trickled by,' Tiffany went on, 'I began to realise that he wasn't getting over it. Melissa,' she sat forward, 'do you know that up until three months ago when I went overseas he was still chasing up leads on you?'

'I . . .'

'And do you realise that for the past nearly three years, he's lived like a monk?'

'I doubt that. I really . . .'

'Well he has, believe it,' Tiffany said forcefully. 'Oh, I'm not saying he hasn't taken someone to bed once in a while. For men that can be about as meaningless as taking someone to the movies except in a purely physical sense. But he's had no affairs, no real association with any woman since you left. Believe me, if he had, I'd have known about it.'

'How could you have . .?'

'I made it my business to know,' Tiffany said bleakly. 'I've got a lot of social contacts, Melissa. I also have, rather had—she's left now—a friend who worked in this very hotel and when Clay moved back here . . . well, suffice to say that you'd be amazed what kind of gossip hotel employees know. But I never found one streak of evidence, one whisper, that he was ever having an affair with anyone.'

'Tiffany . . .' Melissa looked stunned.

Tiffany's lips twisted. 'You're shocked,' she said. 'So was I at first. Shocked at how dogged and determined I could be. But it didn't stop me. And in fact he himself made it easy for me. Because he stayed right here in Sydney. He didn't go overseas, he didn't even go interstate excepting for the trips he made to identify someone who might have been you. He stayed here and from what I was told, what I saw, worked, like a demon. He probably trebled his fortune,' she said with a dry little smile. 'Actually, there was one place he did go . . .' she added very quietly.

'Where?'

'I think that's something you ought to find out for yourself, Melissa,' Tiffany said slowly. 'Ask him where he used to go when he was tired and lonely. And,' she added, 'at the same time why don't you ask yourself another question? Ask yourself this, if you don't call it love when a man is intrinsically faithful to the memory of a girl for three years, what do you call it?'

'I . . .'

'Melissa,' Tiffany said urgently, 'forget about what happened *before* he might have realised what he felt for you. These things happen, believe me . . . And here endeth the lesson,' she said tearfully. 'I won't talk about it again. I'm so happy just to see you . . .'

For a long time after Tiffany had left, Melissa sat staring in front of her. She didn't notice it grow dark, so absorbed was she in her thoughts.

If Tiffany's right, she thought, why hasn't he told me how he feels! Why hasn't *he* told me any of this? Would I have believed him, though? Perhaps not . . . Yet it's hard not to believe Tiffany who was . . . prepared to hate Clay on my behalf and even go to incredible lengths on my behalf to expose him for a bastard. And then there's the other point she raised. Why *does* it hurt so much to think of him with other women . . . yes, even Tanya? Have I been lying to myself for a long time about Clay? Kidding myself . . . but why? There must be a reason . . . oh God! Help me . . .

She jumped convulsively as the door clicked open and the overhead light flicked on, and she turned a white, strained face to the door to see Clay standing there . . .

Melissa drew a breath and her eyes widened because there was something shockingly different about him. His face was pale and the lines beside his mouth deeply scored. And his eyes reminded her, as they had on a day long ago, of frozen water.

'Clay?' she breathed. 'Is something wrong?'

He didn't answer immediately, just stared at her for a very long time and almost as if he'd never seen her before. Then he drawled, 'Oh yes, Melissa. Something so wrong—but I forget, you know all about it. More than I do.' He shut the door carefully. 'Strange, isn't it?' he said and dropped his bag where he stood and strolled over to the bar where he poured himself a straight scotch. 'Strange,' he said again but almost to himself, 'I should have guessed long ago . . .'

He gripped the glass and she noticed that his hand shook. But he lifted it and tossed the contents off. Then he set the glass down very carefully and turned to her. 'Would you like one?'

'Clay—you're drunk!' she said incredulously.

'I wish I was,' he replied and poured two more scotches and brought them over to the settee where she sat. 'I've certainly been drinking but it hasn't been having quite the desired effect,' he murmured as he sat down. 'And what have you been doing today, my sweet wife who hates me?' he queried and raised his glass to her.

'What . . . what do you mean?' she asked feeling suddenly cold. 'Why do you say that?'

He lifted his eyebrows ironically. 'Well, *you've*

said it often enough—oh, I understand why now,' he said with a bitter sort of self-mockery *she* didn't understand. 'In fact I apologise for being so dim,' he added. 'Although if you'd hit me on the head with it, you might have saved us a whole lot of . . . Why didn't you?' he asked with a sudden abrupt directness.

'Didn't what?' she whispered with a curiously hollow feeling at the pit of her stomach.

'Tell me exactly why you hate me so much, Melissa,' he said harshly.

'I . . . don't think I know what you're talking about, Clay . . .'

'We're talking about why you hate me . . . so very much. The real reason. That would have done it, Melissa,' he said and looked at her so piercingly, she knew he wasn't drunk in the accepted sense, although he should have been, she guessed.

'Clay . . .'

'It doesn't matter now,' he said tautly.

'Yes it does. I mean . . . tonight I was going . . . going to . . .' She swallowed and looked away helplessly. What was I going to do tonight. Was I going to . . .? A tiny frown knit her forehead.

'Then you left it a little late,' he interrupted her thoughts. 'Years too late,' he said with a flicker of harshness back in his voice. 'We could have spared ourselves some of this agony at least. But never mind from now on it will be as you wanted. That is,' he said slowly, 'from tomorrow morning . . .'

Her eyes were huge and dark. 'W-what do you mean?'

'I mean, that tonight, I'm going to revive . . . us. You.' A nerve jumped in his jaw but he went on in the same unsteady, husky voice. 'A girl who used to tell me she loved me in a hundred different ways. I'm going to pretend that you never came to hate me, or that I gave you such cause to.' His eyes narrowed and lingered on her lips. 'I'm going to make love to you tonight whether you want me to or not,' he murmured. 'That's not fair to you, is it? But then I don't have a great record of being fair to you, do I?'

She licked her lips and tried to speak but couldn't.

'Don't worry though, it will only be this once and you won't have to hate yourself because you won't have any choice. Oh, and don't worry about saving my soul from sin—I don't think that's possible,' he said with a bitter little smile that cut her to the quick.

'Clay, no, you mustn't . . .'

'Yes I must,' he said very quietly and slid his hand through her hair. 'Don't you understand, this will be the very last time. You'll be free of me after tonight and I'll,' he added barely audibly, 'be free of this torment . . .'

She tried to speak, to tell him that he was wrong, that that's what she wanted to tell him, that she didn't hate him, but he didn't give her a chance. His lips took possession of her mouth and his hands took possession of her body in a way he'd never done before—in a ruthlessly sensual attack that rendered her breathless and gasping and trembling at his every touch.

And when he lifted her bodily into his arms and carried her through to his bedroom, she was too stunned to do anything.

He laid her on the bed and even the way he undressed her was a continuation of that devastating attack on her senses. He slid his hands beneath the silk of her blouse and she shivered with a electric sense of anticipation and moaned in her throat, a tiny sound that trembled in the air between them, a sound of pleasure . . .

Then she was free of her clothes and so was he, and his plundering lips and hands were wandering at will over her body, making her come alive beneath their touch. It was not that he did it brutally, simply that he knew exactly how to arouse her still, and was using every ounce of that knowledge plus all of his skill.

And when she arched her body against him, and whispered breathlessly, yearningly, 'Yes, please, Clay . . .' she knew finally just how much she'd lied to herself. It was not that she'd ever forgotten this, not that she'd ever been able to persuade herself that it had been only a transitory attraction—it was much simpler, she'd only anaesthetised herself against it.

But it was worse. Because when their bodies were still at last, she knew she didn't hate herself. In fact what she felt was quite different. She felt as if she'd come alive after three, long, sleep-drugged years. Burningly, achingly alive, uniquely alive as only Clay could make her feel, like a flower revived by water. And she thought, it *is* like coming home. What a fool I've been. I can never stop loving him, I never did. It doesn't matter what happens, I can't change it . . .

She moved at last and realised she was crying jerkily and her lips moved as she tried to say the words that were in her heart but it seemed impossible to speak. And she didn't see the look of pain in his eyes as he pulled her close to him again and stroked her hair. It was as if the shock of what was almost like being re-born was too great for her. And she fell asleep in a matter of minutes, exhausted, and haunted and frightened by her own ability to deceive herself.

CHAPTER NINE

FOR the second morning in a row, Melissa woke up alone in the penthouse. Woke with a terrible sense of impending disaster, to find a note on the pillow beside her that gave no lie to it.

It was from Clay.

'I know it's futile to say I'm sorry, but I will— for everything. And when you read this, I should be flying out of the country because in view of your father's successful surgery—I spoke to his doctors by phone from Melbourne yesterday— there's no need to continue the pretence of our marriage. But if you'd like to wait until he's stronger before you break the news to him, you could tell him I've had to go overseas on business. He'd understand that. So it's goodbye, Melissa. I can't ask you to forgive me but if you could do one thing for me—try to put this all behind you, and be happy. Also, medical science has worked a small miracle for your father so don't give up hope for yourself. If you haven't seen a gynaecologist recently, please *do it now . . . Clay.'*

'Oh God!' she breathed as the last sentence of the note sank in fully. 'He knew. No . . .' She uttered the word despairingly as she stared wildly at the bedside clock to see that it was nine-thirty. A chaotic jumble of thoughts filled her mind. How did he find out? *That's* what he had meant last night. How could she have slept so late . . . What had happened to breakfast? He must have told them not to disturb her and now ... he'd gone thinking ...

It was a white, suffering face she turned to the door as a loud knocking came at it, and unbelievably, Tanya Miller entered pushing a food trolley and with a bunch of keys dangling from one hand.

'I hijacked these,' she said briefly. 'They tried to tell me you couldn't be disturbed.'

'Tanya?' Melissa breathed, and then everything fell into place—the trip to Melbourne, the way Clay had been last night, the note ... '*You* told him!' she accused. 'About the baby ...'

'To be precise, he tricked me into telling him,' Tanya said grimly. 'Where is he?'

'He's gone,' Melissa said whitely.

'Oh Christ,' Tanya muttered beneath her breath. 'I was afraid of that. That's why I decided to come.'

Melissa stared at her. She was as vivid as ever, Tanya. She wore a wildly shoulder-padded dress with enormous sleeves in a bright green and red stockings and shoes.

'Here,' Tanya said after a tense little pause. She poured a cup of coffee and offered it to Melissa. 'Can I tell you what happened at my end? He arrived out of the blue to see me and I sensed that something was wrong but he merely ... made conversation. Then when I asked how you were, he said—fine, and went on to say something about you confiding in me that day ... I agreed, albeit warily, that you had a bit and he said quite casually, then you know about the baby and how she lost it?'

Melissa made an incomprehensible sound.

'Quite,' Tanya agreed with an ironic glimmer in

her green eyes. 'Now I'm not usually a fool, Melissa, but I assumed if he knew, you must have told him. So I said well, yes, she did. Then he ... I don't know, just something about him when I said that, made me wonder. But I didn't have to wonder for long because he then proceeded to drag the details out of me like ... a police prosecutor,' she said bitterly. 'Of course I got angry and demanded to know what the hell was going on—why he had to come to me for confirmation if he already knew about it. To which he replied, that he hadn't known about it.'

'Then ... how ...?' Melissa stared at her helplessly.

'He said,' Tanya replied, 'that he'd suspected it when he saw you looking at some babies once with such an intense look of pain and grief on your face ... it, well it hit him apparently that the only reason you had to look like that would be if you'd had a baby yourself and lost it ...'

'And what did you tell him?'

'That you were pregnant when you left him but you hadn't realised it. And that you'd lost it and might not be able to have any more ... I'm *sorry*,' Tanya said intensely. She hesitated. 'He also said,' she went on, 'that it would explain the depth of your hatred for him and I knew then, things hadn't worked out as I'd hoped they might. Is that true, Melissa. Do you hate him? And because of that?' Her green eyes probed Melissa's.

'No,' Melissa said huskily. 'I love him—I never stopped.'

'Then why does he think ...' Tanya stopped abruptly. 'Oh I see,' she said slowly. 'You still don't believe he loves you, do you? Well, can I tell you a little story? I wanted to tell you this the last time we talked but it didn't seem to me to be in great ... taste at the time. Nor did I think you really wanted to hear it. But I should have, for two reasons, to set your mind at rest for once and for all about Clay and me and, well ...'

'Tanya,' Melissa whispered. 'I ...'

'Listen, Melissa,' Tanya said very quietly. 'That night, the night before you knocked at my door, after we got home—after Clay had told me about you, he stood at the bedroom window ... just stood there for a long time. So long that I finally asked him what he was thinking about. He didn't turn and I thought he wasn't going to answer. But at last he said—about a little girl who meant more to me than I ever knew ... until it was too late—a girl who was the most lovely, vibrant, shining thing I'd ever had in my life, who used to think I was teaching her so much and never knew how much she taught me ...'

Melissa caught her breath.

Tanya nodded, her green eyes compassionate. 'I said—your wife? He turned to look at me then and there was something in his eyes that ... I don't know, made me want to cry. Then ...' Tanya broke off briefly and looked away but almost immediately, she looked straight back at Melissa. 'A little later he made love to me. But it was different. It was as if I was only nineteen and not long since a virgin instead of,' she shrugged, 'anyway, that's the way it was. And I knew,' she said, 'that in his heart, he was making love to you.'

The silence was complete until Melissa said dazedly, 'He's never told me ...'

'Have you ever shown him that you wanted to hear it?'

'No ...'

'And, I mean the way it happened that day when you knocked on my door, can you understand how he must have felt? Would you have liked to have been in his position? I wouldn't have because it was difficult enough to explain at the best of times but ... my dear, don't cry,' Tanya said gently. 'These things happen ...'

'Yes,' Melissa wept. 'They happen to *me* because that's the kind of fool I am. I have to have other people to spell things out for me. But the worst thing is that I fooled myself for so long. And do you know why? Because I'm no different from my father, after all!' she said passionately. 'To think ... you'd think *I'd* have known better. And now ... it might be too late ...'

'It's never too late, Melissa,' Tanya said forcefully. 'Where's he gone?'

'I don't know. Overseas but ...'

'Well, find out. His office must know. Find out and follow him. Do something positive!'

Later that afternoon Melissa was driving the car Clay had put at her disposal when they'd arrived from Glen Morris, aimlessly through Sydney with her heart and mind almost paralysed. Because, incredibly, Clay's office was as much in the dark as she was. The only communication they'd had from him had been a message to say that he would be advising them of certain changes about to take place, in a few days time.

And all she'd been able to achieve, was a promise—loaded with speculation—from Clay's personal assistant that if he received further word, he'd let Melissa know.

But as she drove through Sydney late that afternoon, a terrible feeling of fear gripped

Melissa's heart. What if Clay had disappeared the way she had, three years earlier?

'But he can't do that, surely!' she said to herself and gripped the steering wheel painfully. 'He can't just walk out on his businesses! Or can he? Perhaps he has some plan to sell them off ... or operate them by remote control, from somewhere where *I* won't ever be allowed to find him?'

She bit her lip hard enough to draw blood at this terrifying thought, and very nearly drove through a red light. And it was only when several irate motorists vented their spleen upon her for her erratic driving that she looked around and made some effort to concentrate on it.

Her idea in going for a drive at all had been to find some secluded, private place where she could get out and walk and breathe some clear, fresh air, and think. Yet as she looked around, she realised with a start, where she was. Darlinghurst ...

She gazed around dazedly at what had been such familiar territory. Only a block away was ...

It wasn't a conscious decision on her part—the car seemed to follow dictates of its own until with no great recollection of parking or stopping, she was nevertheless parked opposite the little terrace house that had been, for such a short while, a haven of unbelievable happiness for her.

She stared across the street and didn't realise her face was wet with tears.

It hadn't changed, not one bit, she saw. It was also occupied, she realised, because there were lights on although it wasn't quite dark yet. And she wondered painfully if Clay had sold it or if it was rented out. Were there strangers using the furniture she'd so lovingly and carefully collected? She'd never had the heart to ask Clay about it ...

But as she stared across the street with pain-filled eyes, the street lights came on and the one opposite her laid a pool of electric blue and silver light on the roof of a car parked beneath it, a long grey car that was exactly like . . .

She stumbled out of her car and across the road.

It *was* Clay's car, it had to be, the upholstery was identical and she knew it had been custom-made for him. She lifted her eyes incredulously to the lighted windows of the house, and her heart started to beat heavily. Was it possible . . .?

Something clicked into place in her mind, something Tiffany had said. Had she meant that he came here when he was tired and lonely?

The front door was not locked. Melissa hesitated for a fraction of a second, then went in.

There was no sign of anyone downstairs as she wandered from room to room in a trancelike daze . . . dazed almost beyond belief because nothing had changed. Everything was exactly as she'd left it, the rug in front of the fireplace, the red-and-white wallpaper in the dining room, the candle-sticks . . .

But it had an air of disuse about it, as if no-one had lived in it for a long time, at least not properly, although there was no dust on any of the surfaces she trailed her fingers along, and the silver was all brightly polished.

Then she heard a sound from above and she jumped and turned towards the staircase, her eyes wide and dark. But there was no further sound and she walked towards the stairs and put her hand on the bannister and breathed deeply.

The door of the main bedroom was ajar and a sliver of light cut the passage carpet diagonally. And the bedroom door made no sound as she pushed it open slowly, no sound at all. So that the occupant of the room didn't stir and she was able to stand in the doorway and drink her fill of him.

It was Clay. He was sprawled in the linen-covered armchair she'd had upholstered to match the curtains, with his head resting back, his eyes closed, one hand shoved into his pocket and the other hanging limply over the arm of the chair. He was wearing a dark suit and a blue shirt but his tie was off and his collar unbuttoned.

Melissa stared. Then her eyes moved to take in the bottle and glass on the small table beside him. And they widened as they moved to the bed and took in a bright, vivid splash of colour that glinted faintly . . . It was her red dress, the one she'd been wearing when she'd first met Clay. And she looked across to the built-in cupboards that lined one wall of the room. Two of the doors were wide open and she saw her clothes hanging there, just as she'd left them.

She swallowed and found her throat hurt. Then she crossed the carpet swiftly and knelt beside the chair.

'Clay?' she said softly.

His eyes flickered open and he frowned but didn't move his head.

'Clay,' she said again, 'it's me . . .'

'*Melissa?*' he murmured, then turned his head to stare down at her as if she was an apparition. And his face paled and he closed his eyes briefly.

'No,' she whispered and started to shake. 'Not Melissa, I've buried her. It's Melly—Melly Forrester, who never stopped loving you and begs you to take her back.'

His knuckles were white as he gripped the arms

of the chair and his mouth pale. 'But she did,' he said barely audibly.

'No,' Melissa said tremulously. 'That wasn't living, that was dying. I died in my heart I think, when I lost your baby because I knew it was my foolish, irresponsible actions that had caused it. That's why I never wanted you to know ... I should never have run away like that—in fact, I wasn't running away from you or my father so much as myself. And do you know why? Because I inherited a Heatley failing, *the* Heatley failing I despised most. Pride ... If I'd been a wiser, different person, I wouldn't have let myself feel— short-changed. I'd have understood that I loved you and nothing could change that. But I allowed pride to tell me otherwise. I couldn't bear to think of you not loving me the way I loved you even though I knew you ... cared in many ways. So I tried to pretend to myself that I hadn't really loved you. And I told myself you'd used me—that made it easier. But it was a lie. Because you never did anything to me that I didn't desperately want you to do. And when I thought I wasn't even thinking of you, that was a lie too. I just couldn't let myself think of you because then I wouldn't be able to hide the truth from myself any more ...'

He didn't say anything for a long time.

'Clay ...?' she faltered at last.

'Oh Melly ...' He said her name for her on a mere breath but it was enough to give her hope. But that slender thread of hope receded with his next words. 'It's too late now,' he said tiredly.

'Why?' she pleaded. 'How can it be if you ... if you love me too?'

'*If* I love you.' His mouth twisted and his eyes

were filled with pain as they rested on her. 'Because I left it too late,' he said with an effort. 'You accuse yourself of pride, but if anyone had cause to act the way you did ...' He shook his head. 'Do you think I don't know that? It was an intolerable thing to do to anyone. But the awful irony of it was, that as soon as I knew you'd gone, I found out what love was. I found out that for me, it was *you*. And that it could only ever be you. Because without you there was a great hole in my life only it was more. It was like a mortal wound that never stopped hurting. I should have known,' he said with a bitter savagery and stared at her with tortured eyes. 'I should have known,' he went on in a lower voice, 'when I had to tell you the truth and knew I'd have given *anything* not to have to watch you ... wilt like a flower in a hailstorm. I should have known when it occurred to me that the old hurts I'd been nursing for so long, suddenly seemed pale and insubstantial and *nothing* compared to what I was doing to you. I should have known when it occurred to me to say—to tell you that I'd fallen in love with you along the way, just in case it was true ...'

'Oh Clay,' she whispered, 'it doesn't matter.'

'Yes it does,' he said starkly.

'Then tell me now ...' The tears were falling fast.

'Melly ...' He reached a hand and touched her wet face gently. 'I saw the way you looked at those babies. I can't ever forgive myself for that. And I can't stand to hear you trying to take the blame for it. Especially when I think of what I plotted and planned to do when I got you back ...'

'None of that matters now,' she wept.

'But it does.' He stroked her hair. 'Let me tell

you . . . When I saw you again for the first time, I wanted to tell you then, desperately. But I could see it was the last thing you wanted to hear, or would believe, and in those circumstances I couldn't blame you. Who could? But it didn't stop me plotting and planning,' he said with a grim, twisted derision, 'Oh no—I thought to myself, if I can just keep her from slipping away again, I can get her back. Well, your father unwittingly lent a hand but I had further plans. Do you know what I planned to do, Melly?' he said harshly. 'I planned to seduce you all over again. And keep on doing it until I got you pregnant. And I thought,' his voice was suddenly exhausted, 'I thought, she won't be able to run away from me then . . .'

The silence was long and heart-stopping as they gazed into each other's eyes. Then Melissa moistened her lips but he spoke first. And she thought she'd never seen so much suffering in anyone's eyes as he said, 'I can *never* forgive myself for that, or for what happened to you. That's why I have to go, don't you see? That's why you have to . . . try to put this all behind you. I don't deserve you, Melly . . . I never did. And I would have been gone,' he added tautly, 'if the bloody flight I was on hadn't developed engine trouble and had to turn back and every other damned flight been booked out until—until . . .' He glanced at his watch and moved sharply.

But she caught his hand. 'Oh thank God,' she murmured and started to kiss it so that her tears mingled with her kisses. 'Oh Clay, don't leave me now,' she wept. 'Don't you see, we've hurt each *other*, but that's all in the past. I love you, that's all that matters now and if you go I'll start to die again . . . don't do that to me. If you leave me now, that will be the one thing you've done to me that I didn't want.'

'Melly ... Melly,' he said in a voice quite unlike his own, and passed a hand wearily over his eyes.

'But don't just take my word for it, let me show you,' she begged with a look of radiant love in her eyes. 'At least let me do that. I can't do it in as many ways as you have—our house, just as I left it, the things I've learnt about you ... so much, but I can do it like this.' She leant forward and put her lips on his and slid her arms around him beneath his jacket. '*Please*,' she whispered against his mouth, 'let me show you.'

'Oh God,' he groaned and gathered her into his arms and began to kiss her with a wrenching tenderness.

Hours later they lay in each other's arms in the lamplit bedroom with their clothes scattered all around, quiet at last and enveloped in the kind of tranquillity that only comes from a great, mutually shared passion. And Melissa thought hazily of the words she'd once said to him ... You do so much for me, she'd said, but I don't do very much for you ...

Well, she'd changed that tonight. Out of a deep well of longing and as if it was the most important deed of her life perhaps, she'd taken the initiative as she'd never done before. She'd set out to love Clay with her hands and her lips, seeking and stroking and loving him, giving herself to him more completely than she'd ever done before but without ever thinking of herself, intent only on pleasing him ...

Yet it had turned out to be the same thing. His pleasure had become hers so that the rhythm of their desire had been like an endless sea, swelling until finally it crashed and splintered into an explosion that had been white hot, and had left him shuddering with the intensity of it as much as she had.

So much so that it was an age before they could speak, a lifetime spent in each other's arms still feeling it wonderingly and so united mentally that words weren't necessary.

Until at last, he moved his chin on her hair. 'You're—I can't find words to describe you,' he said very softly. 'You're the most beautiful person I've ever known.'

She breathed deeply. 'This humble wife is grateful,' she murmured. 'Her heart is in your hands.'

He moved her away so that he could look into her eyes. 'Melly, I *love* you but ...'

'Then,' she said gravely, 'remember what Confucius said. He said that to love and to leave is futile.'

'Confucius,' he answered with a slow smile beginning at the back of his eyes, 'will leap up from his grave one day if we keep misquoting him.'

Her cheek dimpled and he touched it with unsteady fingers. 'Oh God, it's come back,' he said huskily. 'Your dimple—I thought it was gone forever.'

'It's a happy dimple, didn't you know? It needs you, as I do ... Clay?' she said searchingly.

But he didn't answer her in the spoken word. Just pulled her back into his arms as if he'd never let her go ...

CHAPTER TEN

EIGHTEEN months later, Clay spoke into the phone beside Melissa's bed. Ellen Mackenzie was on the other end, a couple of hundred miles away at Glen Morris. And her voice trembled uncharacteristically down the wire.

'A bonny wee boy you say Och ...! And what will you call him?'

'Er ... Patrick,' Clay said apologetically. 'But ...'

'*Patrick!*' Ellen repeated in scandalised tones. 'Where did you get that from, I ask you? Was it your father's name?'

'No, the doctor's. Without him ... but anyway, there's more.' He glanced at Melissa expressively.

'Well, I could have borne James, after his grandfather, I mean I don't hold grudges really, but Patrick ... what do you mean? What could be more than a bonny wee boy?' Ellen demanded.

'A ... bonny wee girl, too,' Clay said.

The silence was palpable. Then Ellen said hoarsely, 'You don't mean twins!'

'Yes I do ...'

'My God!' Ellen said, taking the Lord's name in vain for perhaps the first time in her life. 'I'll be right on the next plane. My poor baby! You tell her I'll be right there! And what will you call t'other?'

Clay looked faintly alarmed but dealt with each statement in reverse order. 'Flora. And Melissa is fine, really she is. So there's no need for you to

185

come up and anyway, as soon as they're released from hospital, I'll be bringing them all down to Glen Morris at their father and grandfather's express invitation—that is, if you think you can cope with us all?'

Ellen snorted and delivered herself of a scathing address on the subject to which Clay listened with an amused smile. But she did finish by saying, 'Flora, eh? Now that's what I call a good name!'

'Thought you might,' Clay murmured, and after they'd exchanged farewells, he put the phone down and turned to Melissa, who was laughing weakly.

'She wanted to come up,' he said wryly. 'I've seen what she can do to an hotel!'

'I know,' Melissa said feelingly. 'But I had to laugh too, at the way you said you'd be bringing "them all down"—as if overnight, we've grown into an army.'

'I suspect we have, my darling,' he replied with his lips quirking. 'My very own army . . .' He sat down on the bed beside her and drew her into his arms. 'You were magnificent,' he said into her hair.

'Only because you were there to help me,' she whispered.

He held her close. 'How do you feel?'

'Tired . . . and sore. But so very happy!'

'So do I. I . . .' He held her away from him and looked lingeringly and lovingly down at her pale, weary face, 'you've never been so beautiful as you are now. And I feel as if I've given you back . . . something I once took from you.'

A shimmer of tears came to her lavender-blue eyes. But she said softly, 'Thank you for the first part. But you're wrong about the second part. What was lost, *we* lost. And what's been gained, we've gained, only,' her lips trembled into a smile, 'because we never seem to do anything in half measures, we've gained doublefold!'

'And who,' he said as he took her face in his hands, 'do you attribute those words of wisdom to?'

'Me!' Her cheek dimpled.

He smiled back lovingly and bent his head to kiss her.

Share the joys and sorrows of real-life love with
Harlequin American Romance!™

GET THIS BOOK FREE as your introduction to Harlequin American Romance — an exciting series of romance novels written especially for the American woman of today.

Mail to:
Harlequin Reader Service

In the U.S.
2504 West Southern Ave.
Tempe, AZ 85282

In Canada
P.O. Box 2800, Postal Station A
5170 Yonge St., Willowdale, Ont. M2N 6J3

YES! I want to be one of the first to discover
Harlequin American Romance. Send me FREE and without obligation *Twice in a Lifetime.* If you do not hear from me after I have examined my FREE book, please send me the 4 new **Harlequin American Romances** each month as soon as they come off the presses. I understand that I will be billed only $2.25 for each book (total $9.00). There are no shipping or handling charges. There is no minimum number of books that I have to purchase. In fact, I may cancel this arrangement at any time. *Twice in a Lifetime* is mine to keep as a FREE gift, even if I do not buy any additional books.   154 BPA BPGE

Name	(please print)	

Address		Apt. no.

City	State/Prov.	Zip/Postal Code

Signature (If under 18, parent or guardian must sign.)

This offer is limited to one order per household and not valid to current Harlequin American Romance subscribers. We reserve the right to exercise discretion in granting membership. If price changes are necessary, you will be notified.

AMR-SUB-1R

INDULGE IN THE PLEASURE OF SUPERB ROMANCE READING BY CHOOSING THE MOST POPULAR LOVE STORIES IN THE WORLD

Longer, more absorbing love stories for the connoisseur of romantic fiction.

An innovative series blending contemporary romance with fast-paced adventure.

Contemporary romances—uniquely North American in flavor and appeal.